The Mango

and other stories

The Mango War

and other stories

MARTIN
MALONE

NEW
ISLAND

THE MANGO WAR AND OTHER STORIES
First published 2009
by New Island
2 Brookside
Dundrum Road
Dublin 14

www.newisland.ie

ISBN 978-1-84840-035-1

Book design by Inka Hagen

Printed in Ireland by ColourBooks.

New Island receives financial assistance from The Arts Council (An Comhairle Ealaíon),
Dublin, Ireland

10 9 8 7 6 5 4 3 2 1

Contents

Acknowledgments

RTÉ Radio 1, BBC Radio 4, BBC
World Service and the Belgian
and Dutch national radio stations
broadcast versions of some of
these stories. Other versions
appeared in *The Fiddlehead*
(Canada), *The Bridport Anthology*
(UK), *Phoenix Irish Short Stories
2000*, *The Dublin Review*, *The Stinging Fly*, *The Dublin Quarterly*, *The
Sunday Tribune*, *FISH*, *Books Ireland*
and *WP Monthly*.

'The Mango War' won RTÉ's Francis MacManus 2004
Short Story Competition (adjudicators: Dermot Bolger,
Anne Enright and Colm Tóibín).

'You See It So Clearly' won the 2004 Killarney
International Short Story Award.

God of Little

He lurks outside the multi-storey car park, looking up at its roof. He looks in my direction then, and starts to walk towards me. I'm fiddling with a bunch of keys to the roller shutters. My thoughts are on the yellow skip bin outside the Control Lodge and how it smells worse than it did yesterday. Intended for builders' rubble only, it now holds mattresses, sofa cushions and household rubbish, left there by people not afraid to take advantage.

There's a misty rain falling. The sort of rain that wets you without your noticing. He asks if there's a McDonald's in the mall and I say there's a Burger King; that McDonald's are up town by the traffic lights, across from Woodie's. I tell him the mall won't open for another twenty minutes.

He's about thirty and there isn't an ounce of bother in his face.

'I'll wait around,' he says. 'I'm as hungry as a condemned man.'

'Are you?' I say. 'I have cheese sandwiches – do you want one?'

'Ah Jesus, no man – no thanks. That's your lunch, I couldn't.'

He saunters away then, pulling up the hood on his grey hoodie, lips clutching at a cigarette.

The shutters automatically rise, rusty bones grinding and groaning after the night's sleep. In the Lodge I check the float and open the register. I then examine the diagnostic panel on the screen – Pay Station 61 has a red X over it. This machine hasn't worked for yonks, even after repair and servicing. It wants nothing to do with people and money. Some people are hard of sight, however, and fail to read the 'Out of Order' sign displayed on the machine's screen, so we had to tape over the ticket and payment slots. Gag them, so to speak.

Next I make tea and read over the computer print-out of yesterday's takings, to determine if any of the machines need emptying of notes or coins. The coin and note boxes in the machines are known as vaults. I'm a senior car-parking host and the guys on my team are known as parking hosts. Sounds like we're cattle who ingest some sort of worm.

Andy's my second-in-command. He is a pleasant man, quiet, and fond of his tipple. He doesn't wear his false teeth and so his lips have caved in. He's forever skint and asking me to sub him from petty cash.

The mornings are quiet in the car park. Mornings are when we do our cleaning and counting and bitching. After which one of the hosts will tour the pay stations and lobbies and different zones for one last look round before the herd return to feast on the grazing fields that is the shopping mall.

Junkies occasionally shoot up in the upper levels of the car park, hidden in corners, leaving behind blood, faeces, spent needles. We have the kit for that: the powder that acts like a cast on the shit, the heavy-duty cleanser that does for the blood. Always I have to remind the team to spray the spoiled area with odour neutraliser before cleaning the mess – bugs are airborne and the job just isn't worth taking the risk with your health.

We get all sorts: kids, hobos, druggies – but they don't cause us half the aggro that some customers do.

For instance, we often change flat tyres for people who don't say thanks – let alone give a tip. We open doors where keys have been locked in cars; assist people in finding where they've parked their cars; kick-start dead batteries to life.

Retrievers are those who carry tickets in their mouths. They pluck the ticket from the dispenser, the barrier lifts and they drive through with their ticket clamped between their lips – where it remains as they search for a parking space. Retrievers, when they've finished their shopping, go to an automatic pay station to pay the tariff and end up buzzing the Lodge. Usually they say something like 'The machine says my ticket won't work'. The machine doesn't say this – what reads on its screen is 'Card faulty'. The customer says it like it's the machine that's to blame – but the fault lies with a moist ticket. As the company I work for prides itself on its the-customer-is-always-right orientation, I never mention that their oral intimacy with an inanimate object is to blame for the machine's failure to read their ticket. They might misconstrue my meaning as innuendo – that there might be something Freudian about this clamping of a ticket between their lips, some in-built canine instinct – and take offence.

The Control Lodge is our nerve centre; I have CCTV cameras and intercom, computers. I run the show. I can let people exit without charge, if I want. Sometimes I do. I am God of this world. It is little of which to be God. But it is better to be a God of Little than nothing.

Our multi-storey car park comprises both the Red Zone – so called because of its red walkways – and the Green Zone, including the basement and its green walkways. Both the Red and the Green Zones are lettered and numbered on their pillars. The Green Zone is a vast apron of an area, configured with multiple traffic corridors and two lobbies with lifts, escalators and pay stations. People get lost.

The pay stations are also numbered. Tall, chubby, yellow machines, state-of-the-art we were told by the manufacturer. They break down frequently, which I suppose is what state-of-the-art machines do best.

We charge twenty euro for a lost ticket. But we have some discretion; it's a personal call. If the person is genuine and it looks like twenty euro is a lot of money to them, badly needed, we let them out without charge. Usually I can tell by their tone of voice if they're spoofing. I've probably been duped a few times, but the way I see it is this – I'd sooner be duped than screw someone who'd maybe been headed home wondering where the hell she'd gone wrong, not being able to afford things she'd seen in the shops.

Like people, we get the best and the worst of cars in here. We've had cars abandoned here, a couple of motorbikes. Not crocks either, but what a lot of people would consider a fine mode of transport, and others would call a basic car. I suppose it depends on whether you're buying your first car or upgrading. People used to having a car forget what it's like to walk and the times they wished they owned a car.

We call in the registration numbers to the cops and if the vehicle has been used in the perpetration of a crime, they take it away. Head Office in Dublin decides what to do about the others.

Women will usually tell you they are lost and can't find their car – they have the sense to do this. Invariably they will not know the registration number of the car – I'll be given the colour and the make and, if I am lucky, a digit or two. From this scant information I am expected to conjure up their lost vehicle. The entry-point number printed on their ticket is also a help in tracking down these 'lost' cars. When it is found, they always sigh with relief – afraid that their car had been stolen – and the strain leaves their features. One lady even insisted on tipping me with a ten euro note, which left my lips flapping wordlessly.

Men, on the other hand, will spend forty minutes or more searching for their car, sooner than admit to anyone that they are lost. I let them walk. Old people I help find their car because they are banjaxed from walking after about ten minutes into the search, and my mum is elderly and I wouldn't like to think of her lost in a subterranean car park.

This morning I see the woman on the monitor. Done up to the nines. A gorgeous woman, she sticks her ticket in the machine and looks at the price register on the screen, then presses the cancel button. I see her look at the ticket and drop it into a waste bin that has advertisement stickers for the new *Die Hard* movie on its side panels.

I radio Andy to bring me the ticket in the bin at the entry to the lifts at Green Zone A.

'Hunky dory,' he says.

I wish he'd think of saying 'Yes' or 'OK' or something else.

Five minutes later the stylish dresser is at the Lodge window grille, her eyes full of tears.

'I've lost my ticket,' she says.

'That'll be twenty euro,' I say.

'I'm not paying twenty euro.'

'That's what it costs.'

'I'm in a hurry – I've got to go to a funeral. I can't be late.'

I shrug one shoulder. 'You're going to be later if you don't pay.'

There's no funeral, but she'd said so, and now can't go back on it. So she pays and when she's gone, Andy says, 'Jesus, you were very hard on her.'

I show him the ticket he'd handed me and insert it then in the manual-cashier. It registers as a ten-euro tariff.

'It's her ticket,' I say.

'Aw, you were right, so.'

Next thing, I dunno – it's sort of a blur. Like something you'd see in a movie where a guy falls down the side of a skyscraper, dropping by the windows of offices or apartments. Some people noticing, most of them not. Anyhow this lad zips by our window and lands in the skip full of builder's rubble and old piss-stained mattresses.

'Jesus!' Andy says, looking at me to see if what he'd seen was real.

Andy says 'Jesus' in response to just about anything, but this had more depth. Like a real prayer. The guy with the grey hoodie eases himself out of the skip. He has a tight haircut and wears blue jeans – all of him is coated with builder dust.

Andy says, 'He's alive! Can you credit that? A miracle.'

We step out of the office and go out front to see if there is something we can do to help him. I wonder if he'd jumped or was thrown.

These days with so much violence going round it's hard to tell. The fella is in a hurry to be somewhere. He half-walks, half-stumbles past an exit barrier and goes on to push through the white double-doors into a hall that leads to the lifts and a stairwell up to the Red Zone and an exit on to an avenue. 'Will one of us go after him?' Andy says.

'Where's he going, do you think?' I say.

'I dunno.'

We look up at the side of the multi-storey. A long, long drop – seven levels, fourteen car-park floors. 1A, 1B … and so on.

'I wonder what level he came down from?' Andy says.

'Hardly the top one, do you think?'

'Jesus!' Andy says.

This time we see him leap over the parapet – third or fourth level. This time he misses the skip. We hear the slap.

Andy runs and gets a tarpaulin from the store to cover the body, while I go and kneel by the guy and say a prayer for him. The thing you do when there's nothing else you can do for someone. A jittery prayer with my stomach halfway up my throat.

Andy and I dislike the hoodie man and what he did. See, he didn't give us a chance to give him his money back, or deal with his complaint – whatever it was.

It's gone so that it's getting hard to be even a God of Little in this world.

The Date

A girl with an artificial eye took my order for fried chicken wings and chips. Friendly sort with a smile, hurried off her feet. She asked if I wanted my coffee now or with my meal. I said, 'Now, please,' seeing as the place was packed and the meal could be a while coming.

I was to meet a forty-year-old, separated, blind date called Marie, who in her ad said she wanted to meet someone with a good sense of humour and who didn't mind being with a smoker. She didn't show – OK, it happens. I gave her fifteen minutes over the appointed and mutually agreed time, outside the mall. Maybe she took stock from a distance and didn't like the cut of me, and right now is putting distance between herself and the mall before she calls.

I could look a little like her ex. That might be it. My first girlfriend after my divorce bore an uncanny resemblance to my ex-wife. There the contrast ended – though it was like comparing a tiger to a kitten, y'know – as my ex had a tongue like one of those light sabres in *Star Wars* and a look that'd wither a thistle. The

9

freezer we kept in the garage had more human warmth. Arctic cold – get the picture?

Easy to tell we didn't part on good terms – she got everything: the house, the car, the kids, the TV. I left them all behind, getting out before she killed me. A hell zone – that's what our marriage was.

So the girl with the eye landed my coffee in front of me with a smile. The mug's three-quarters full – what's she saying? That I look sort of incontinent?

I didn't like sitting up at the counter, but it was either that or join the queue for a table. All I could see from there were girls running about taking and delivering orders. Wearing these mauve baseball caps and white T-shirts – too Americanised if you ask me. A coloured girl with braided hair, very slim, very attractive, sidled up to the girl with the eye and said something that drew a smile. Lovely smile. I mean you'd think the sun and moon had gotten together, or there'd been a collision of stars.

She caught me looking and fired up red about the cheeks. I reddened too – knew right off what she was thinking: she was thinking that I'd focused on her eye. I read the duplicate of the bill she had given me. Ali – nice name.

When she delivered the chicken wings I said she had a lovely smile. I said it quickly with a smile. She smiled back but didn't redden. I copped the ring on her finger then. Married. I envied the guy she was married to – just for the smile.

Ate up and had another coffee – this time the mug came full. Then I did something I had told myself I wouldn't do. Went back outside the mall – casual, like I was just browsing that way and not looking out for anyone or anything in particular. I didn't know what to do when I saw Marie. She was as she had said she would be, in a black leather jacket, standing right of the door, dangling her car keys. She was thinner, shorter and older than I had envisaged. Her hair long and dyed black with copper streaks that lost her points in my book. I don't like women who carry out a full-scale assault on their age – that sort of battle needs tact, decorum and a frustrated awareness that victory is impossible.

'Marie?' I said.

She looked my way, up a little. God, she was short. Not quite dwarf small, but close. Pretty face, lean, lips a red wet look. Thin trails around her eyes showed where the battle was losing ground the most. Perfect teeth. Too good to be all her own. Her large grey eyes revealed very little of what she was thinking. Though I bet she thought I was taller, heavier and not as handsome as she had hoped. I'd lost a stone and shaved off the beard in recent weeks. Let the hair grow a little longer, considered dyeing it but decided not to when I remembered my dad and how the ceiling of his car always held a black spot of dye.

'Gerry?'

I nod.

'Sorry for being late but—' she said.

11

'It's OK.'

'My mobile was flat so I couldn't call – the traffic …'

Long pause.

'Coffee?' I said awkwardly.

'Yes, sure – there's a nice place at the top of the escalators.'

We moved through the mall. I said the weather was bad for this time of the year and she agreed. She kept moving the strap of her shoulder bag back on her shoulder every time it slipped – this was often by the time we sat in by the panoramic windows that looked out at the vast car park. There had been a car crash at a roundabout – where a police car's blue lights now cut through the persistent drizzle.

I paid for the cappuccinos and she for the muffins. We're going Dutch, she said. The insisting she did at the till embarrassed me. Fingers foraging coins from her black purse, like the claw in an amusement arcade where you try to pinch a furry rabbit from a pile of them. She bought the chocolate chip ones. I said they were messy and went back up to the service counter and got some more serviettes. I didn't know yet that she licked her fingers. A habit that messed about with my nerves. I told her where I lived and what I did to earn a crust. Saying I drove a bulldozer in a county-council tip-head. Smelly job but the pay was good.

She said she worked in a dry-cleaners and put in some extra hours in the local chipper to pump up her earnings a bit. I said I was kidding about working in the dump. I'm a gardener, horticulturist, y'know. Work nights for my brother on the weekend – he's got his own security firm.

'That's nice, but why did say you were working in a dump?' she said.

I shrugged. 'A joke – trying to be smart – sorry.'

'My father worked in the council dump.'

'Oh.'

'He never thought it was a joke.'

'I didn't know.'

'How could you have?'

I'd blown it. Nice little thing, firm breasts under her jacket. I hadn't made up my mind about her until it looked like I had lost her.

'Start again?' I said.

'Best of four chances – is it?'

'Have I blown two already?' What else I wondered? Shit …

She went on to say that she had two kids, twins aged seven, and that she had been married to a guy in the army. She said she could never bring herself to call him a soldier. He drank a lot, could be violent. Never showed remorse but blamed her instead for provoking him.

I listened hard, really hard. All the time thinking how natural it appeared for her to open up, to sketch out her history, leaving me in no doubt what she was driving at – she didn't want history to repeat itself.

'Where is he now?' I asked.

'Down the country, living with his mum – he tried to kill himself last year – they blame me, y'know? His family.'

The rail-track of frowns between her eyebrows suddenly deepened. She continued, 'Not one of them came to see me when he put me in hospital. I almost died from the hiding that he dished out.'

Then she drew a breath and said, 'Your turn.'

'My turn?'

'Yes, *Quid Pro Quo*, like Hannibal in *Silence of the Lambs* – it's the only Latin I know.'

She smiled. First real one.

I told her that I didn't hit people, but that I understood how a man might raise his hand to a woman. It didn't make it right, of course. Catherine had had a fiery temper, short fuse and she was demanding. If she didn't get what she wanted she sulked. She measured herself against what other people had, and if she fell short she nagged until she had me put it some way right. I came to realise that nothing I did was ever going to be enough for her – and then one June morning she pounded up the stairs about eleven and shouted for me to get up.

Like I was only two hours in bed after coming off night shift. She kept calling and calling though until eventually I got up. But when I did, I showered and began to pack while all the time she kept daring me to go, saying I hadn't the balls. If the kids had been there I wouldn't have left, but they weren't and I walked out. Sleep wasn't the issue – I didn't sleep for three nights after I moved out. So I walked and I've been walking since then. Sometimes it gets so I want to turn around and go home, but she wouldn't have me back – she's got a Don Juan in now, or cuckoo, whatever you call a rat in another man's nest – which is, peculiarly enough, what I've occasionally been since – 'but there you are, Marie, enough to be going on with, yeah?'

She held her mug with all her fingers and stared over the brim at me.

'How long are you divorced?'

'Two years.'

'You still have a lot of scars.'

'They're healing.'

'And you're willing to take a chance on love again?'

'Aren't you?'

'Yes, I suppose I am.'

Something in her tone, however, suggested I wasn't going to be her next port of call. I wanted her in a physical way, but that wasn't going to happen. She couldn't wait to get away. I was cruel and bought two more cappuccinos and muffins, complete with sufficient serviettes – but she licked her fingers again anyway. When she finished, she asked if I'd mind her smoking and I shook my head. She slid her chair back and crossed her short legs. The ends of her jeans had a frilled pattern of roses about the ankles. There was a strip of gum on the upper sole of her brown shoe.

She traced the nib of a finger around her lower lip, and panned the floor like someone weighing up an escape route.

'So, what do you think, Marie – do we go further or leave things at the preliminaries – say well met and hail and all that?'

I wanted her to say it out straight, because I knew she wanted to be kind and subtle.

'It's hail fellow, well met, isn't it?'

'Don't know – but you understand what I mean – that's the main thing, isn't it?'

'It is, sure.'

She stretched her lips and stubbed her cigarette in the ashtray. The sort of things people do when they have something bad to tell you – bad for you, but not for them. Telling you is the bad part for them – getting it done with. After that it's a relief.

'I understand,' I said, when she had unburdened herself.

'It's nothing personal,' she said.

It was. But I said nothing.

I wasn't too disappointed. This happens. I've had to do the same a couple of times. It's never easy. And the reason for shaking the head mightn't be clear-cut; you just work on instinct, which is weird in a way, because instinct is to blame for all the love trouble in the first place.

She weaved through the tables and chairs, mounted the escalator and disappeared. Left nothing behind except a cigarette butt, two mugs of half-finished cappuccinos and reams of unused serviettes.

Lake of Dreams

We are in France, mobile-homing it down south in a place called Le Lac de Rêves, near Montpellier, when my father tells my mother he's leaving her. He doesn't mention leaving me. This is typical of him.

It didn't come as a great surprise to her. Its timing did though. But his intentions weren't to spoil the holiday. He blamed the Kronenbourg in his veins for loosening his thoughts.

Mother said he'd always find someone or something else to blame. We know there's another woman involved. Her name's Cindy and she's a secretary in Father's solicitors firm.

She's tall, red-headed and pencil-skinny. I've met her once, her green eyes measuring me when I called into Father's office. She speaks with a put-on upper-class accent. Mother says she's a common slut. A gold-digging tramp. Mother told me that she'd insisted on travelling here on holiday. She thought that a long distance between him and Cindy would cool their relationship, but he's never off the telephone, spending a fortune on phone cards.

Mother said he must be the first man ever to get a letter from home while on holiday abroad.

We're sitting on a sun-baked bench facing the Lake of Dreams. There's a stand of pink flamingos just beyond the mudflats, where the brochure warns people not to venture. Mother is quiet. We smell of sun cream and lip balm.

Mother apologises for Father. She says I shouldn't be having my childhood intruded upon. She looks at me as though she is blameless in all of this. She is deceiving herself, for they are equally to blame for having, what they tell their friends is, 'a problem child' on their hands.

I am a problem because they have always seen me as one. A calendar marking their age, a rope tying up their freedom. I'm thirteen, with big feet getting bigger. I spend most of my time in the pool. I like to look at the bronzed ladies and their naked breasts. But the novelty's wearing off after a week and I don't look at breasts anymore unless they're exceptionally large.

I haven't got much of a tan. My arms and shoulders have, that's all. I have to use lots of after-sun lotion. I tell Mother not to concern herself with Father. Loads of fellows in my boarding school have the same problem – either a father or a mother is missing. Nothing in life is complete.

Mother takes the sun quite easily. It pours over her. But then she has a sunbed at home, and she lies on it most days. She's slim, too. She rides an exercise bike and when I'm at home I wake to its whirring noise from the small gym Mother has set up for herself in the utility room.

She wants to know if I understand what's going on. She says that sometimes people fall out of love with each other, and they meet someone else ... and the rest is nature. She's looking as usual at her painted toenails as she's speaking, as though they are the target for her words. I feel like telling her that if she spoke to Father instead of her toenails, she'd still have him, or at least he'd know she was trying in earnest to reach him.

The lake waters are a deep blue, and a certain indistinguishable perfumed smell travels on the warm breeze coming from there. While Mother looks at her toenails I take in the ants. Long columns of large ants carrying morsels of food to their home, disappearing in the red earth's myriad cracks.

We took the ferry to France. Father doesn't like sailing, didn't like sharing a cabin with Mother and complained of the menu prices, the noise of the ship's engines, the fact that every snotty-nosed child in Ireland seemed to be on the vessel. I thought it was brilliant. The entertainment was great, and the food was good, and Mother enjoyed the trip, too. Father likes to moan. He always moans. But never about himself.

Father is lean and solemn-faced. He lifts weights, and plays squash. He sits by the pool all day wearing his Ray-Bans, sun creaming himself, wearing his designer shorts and expensive gold chains around his neck and wrist. Mother says he should be on the lake with the flamingos.

We're staying in a large mobile home called an Elegance. I have a room to myself, Mother too, while Father sleeps in the living area. At night I visit each of them. Both are either preening themselves or looking in the mirror in search of protruding ear or nostril hairs. Father sometimes fondles a beer can. He has jet-black hair he keeps gelled and slicked back. When he's not looking at himself, he's taking in the pool ladies. I don't think Cindy would be pleased if she saw that.

Mother doesn't mind. She passes remarks on Frenchmen and their tiny bottoms. Cindy isn't a patch on the beauties here. Mother says she'd be like a red cabbage alongside roses. I understand why Mother would say something like that.

She tells me it'll be great. I'll have two homes to visit – hers and Father's. I think Mother is under the impression that the boarding school is my real home. I tell her I already feel like a dog that's been sent to a kennels while his masters go away on holiday. The only thing is – the dog's masters forget to collect him when they return off holiday. Mother looks at her toenails and says I'm being silly.

I don't think they like having me around. Father can't believe I have such big feet. He makes me feel as though I'm a freak.

Mother doesn't like cooking or washing my clothes, and doesn't like hiring someone to do both for me.

Grandmother used to complain about her unmotherly ways, and Mother would buck up her notions a little. But Grandmother died last year.

In her will she asked to be cremated, which I thought was cool at the time, and very brave of her. She left me a little money and a small cottage no one has lived in for a long, long time. I might live there when I leave boarding school, then again I might not. I like sketching. I sketch all the time.

Mother and Father say my sketchings are 'nice'. They like the ones of the flamingos on the lake. They don't like the ones I do of them. I put in too many wrinkles, especially about the eyes. This hurts them. I think it's the only way I can hurt them.

The sketch I did of a shark in the pool is Father, though he doesn't know. The shark wears a chain around his fin and a smile to show his sharp teeth. The woman he's standing above is Cindy, though I've given her smaller breasts. I suspect that this would hurt her.

Our first night off the MV *Normandy* we stayed in a mobile home in Les Étangs Fleuris, outside Paris. Father got lost heading there, and it took numerous attempts to get back on the right track. He said he was used to seeing Paris from the air and through the window of a hotel room. Mother said that this was quite true, but that he'd been in Paris a fortnight ago and could have planned the route a little better, if he'd left his hotel room. Father glanced at Mother. He didn't know till then that she knew about his Paris weekend with Cindy.

Eventually we got on the A86 and took Exit 13 leading us to a roundabout pointing in the right direction. Later that evening Father skirted round his red 04 BMW and checked for stone markings or scrapes. Mother and Father have a tendency to care for things that have no feelings.

We left for EuroDisney early the next morning. Once there, Mother said Father walked around it as though he'd visited it before. I liked Frontierland best, with the fort, its pencil-topped walls, the covered wagons. I tried to sketch a cannon by the fort's entrance, but I got shoved too many times, so I hope to work from the photographs when they're developed. Phantom Manor was brilliant and so, too, was the Pirate ride. I liked the idea of the Thunder Mesa. If you looked at that alone, your imagination could take you straight to the Wild West.

We drove through the Pyrenées mountains to get here. Signposts warned of wolves and deer. I saw fields of sunflowers. Smiling flowers. I thought of Van Gogh and his missing ear. Hang gliders flitted in the skies like colourful moths. Later we stopped in Millau and bought chips from a van. All the while the silence between Mother and Father was murderous. Father resented being dragged on holiday and Mother resented the reason she'd to come on holiday: to drive a wedge between Cindy and Father.

In the confined spaces of the mobile home it's impossible for them to ignore each other. The sun is too hot in the mornings to lie out. They try very hard to be civil towards each other. But I sense that they are living on the edge of their nerves. That one is going to lash out at the other.

Mother's temper is frightening. The alarm clock narrowly misses Father's head. Mother screams and Father shouts. They say terrible things to each other. They forget I am listening. They forget I am here. They find me easy to forget.

I sketch. The mobile shakes because of Father's slamming doors and stomping feet. Mother is crying in the living area, holding her hands to her face. Father's BMW takes its leave of us. He goes, not having said goodbye.

It is what I expected to happen.

Later, Mother comes out of her room and says we should pack. We're flying home. I don't mind. I don't like the insects, the relentless sun, the mobile home's cramped space, the fact that I was expected to live on fruit and breakfast cereals alone. The fact that my arms and neck are burned, that I can't sketch because of the heat, can't lose myself from them.

They give me money. It is money they don't need, it is money they intend me to spend and in the spending to keep away from them. I can do what I like with this money. In the boarding school it ensures I have plenty of friends. We take a plane home from Montpellier. It's early morning as the ground drops away. I imagine I see Father's BMW turning back into the camp. It would be

23

so easy to spot because of its garish red colour, but I know he believes he has nothing to come back to, and therefore will keep going until he reaches Cindy.

We'll be home before him and Mother will bad-mouth him to everyone. It is the way.

I don't leave any note a week later at home. I leave them my sketches of the holiday instead: an angry man standing on his toes, pointing his finger. A woman sitting on the edge of the sofa with her hands to her head. A broken alarm clock, its batteries spilled. A boy sitting on the edge of lake waters, looking at the red sun slowly sinking. The water lapping at his toes.

The Gift Taken Back

They discovered that Billy was deaf the day the truck reversed into him; within weeks Billy, who was seven back then, had gone from being a bright kid to one whose mind seemed never there. But then the truck business cleared the matter up. Billy wasn't going stupid the way Grandad did last year before he died. Poor Grandad spoke about things he never would've if the lights had been on in his head, but golly there was a mega power cut and all his secrets spilled out, and worse thing was he didn't know he'd no more secrets left and kept right on talking, like a needle stuck on an old record player. Over and over. We got to hear about Busty Lisa in New Orleans, Rosy Mae in Manhattan, Vicky Long Tongue in Vancouver and Camel Delahunty with the two front humps in Dallas, originally from Newbridge in Ireland. The stuff he was saying about them was nice, but dirty. All their names tumbled out like the hair I imagined falling from their shoulders, and with each name the other gran's face would fold the way Grandad used to fold his newspaper.

Dad said little, just called Grandad a tiny horny whore under his breath, but saying it in a good way, like he had a sort of admiration and envy for him. The other gran cried a lot but was OK afterwards when Reverend Thackaberry pointed out that Grandad had chosen to die in her bed, no one else's. A silver cloud on the horizon for the other gran, I suppose, but the fact was that he could only die in the one bed and it probably would have cost him money to die in the likes of Camel Delahunty's. Grandad was mean with money, both grandads were – Dad said they were thinking of ways to bring their stashes with them when they kicked the bucket.

Anyway we was all worried that Grandad had passed on some of his lost marbles to Billy, and Thank All the Hot Shit in Hell, Dad said, that he was only deaf and not stupid. Billy was standing there with his back to a reversing truck; all of us were moving because that reversing noise that big trucks make was telling us to, but there was our Billy – and he hearing nothing. The doctor devoured my parents. He said they should have wised up months ago to Billy's ear problem. Dad said he thought Billy was ignoring them and that this was a hormonal pre-teenagey thing. Mam said the doctor said it was a genital disease. Gran said, 'Wha?' and Mam said it louder, 'A genital disease.'

Dad sighed from the sofa and moaned, 'It's a CON-genital disease.'

'All the same,' Mam said.

'It's not.'

'It's inher– inher– You know what I mean – boils down to genitals in the end, doesn't it?'

Dad's eyebrows did a traffic jam. 'We'll have to make sure Billy gets to sign-language school.'

'My Billy isn't going to any special school.'

'He has to.'

'In my ass.'

I guess that's where the rows started in the house. They got worse. My two grans and my living grandad (though you wouldn't know it sometimes) sort of did a United Nations thing and made the matter worse. The living grandad slopped his lips together before he ever said a word. Everyone would wait, thinking he was about to make an important announcement that would settle all the rows, but all he'd come out with was 'When's dinner?' or 'What time is it?' Stupid things. I couldn't wait to hear that old boy's secrets.

Billy said in our room one night, 'Mac … did you let a fart?'

'I thought you were deaf?' I said, pointing to an ear.

'I can still smell, you know?'

'I didn't think of that.'

He got out of bed and opened a window. A wiry scut of a boy in his baggy boxers, he stood looking at the moon, its grey moonscape we used to think was the face of a man, and the stars the dead grandad loved. A cold breeze stirred the curtains, and after a few moments Billy got back in his bed. I could tell he'd been crying because he pretended to be brushing his fringe out of his eyes. He'd fair hair like me, except his was a dirtier colour. He was the dead granddad's favourite. I was the favourite of no one, not even a dead person. Dad said I was too strong-minded for anyone to warm to. Strong-minded. I'm not, I don't think. But because Billy was sad I didn't let any more farts that night, even though I sure as hell wanted to, but farting in a deaf person's company is like shooting someone in the back.

Over the toast in the morning the argument raged.

'He's not going to no dumb school,' Mam said.

I often wondered how anyone so pretty could be so stupid. And I wondered more how Dad didn't flake her chin like Jethro Morphy down the road a bit did to his missus. His missus was tamed, truly tamed, but she was real unhappy; carried a permanent frown in her mid-forehead and her hazel eyes were always weepy. Her face hadn't been marked for some weeks now, and she looked sort of well, Dad noted, without the make-up. He meant without the black eye and puffed lip.

But he reckoned the makeup would be back when Jethro got out of prison. Mrs Morphy knew a bit of sign language, having worked in the kitchen of a deaf school. Dad asked her to teach Billy the basics, but she just looked through him and murmured OK.

Billy told me that she sat him down and made these wild gestures with her hands, her fingers acting looney, like they were little pups she couldn't train. In the end he started laughing and she was laughing too, until

Jethro showed his face, holding the Morphy twins by their tiny hands. Jethro was a human bear, grizzly-bearded with high cheeks that highlighted his blood pressure. Billy sensed that the man was really bad, and he got the weirdest feeling that something shitty was going to happen in that house.

The doc called round and explained a bit more about Billy's deafness, how it had been stealing up on him since he was a babe. The other gran, the one with the dead grandad, said, 'That bitch of a mother of his won't let Billy go to the deaf school.'

The doc didn't want to get involved. You could see by him. He got real uptight and nervous. Someone had shot at him before when he'd intervened in a family dispute. In Oregon, I think.

'No school,' Mam said.

The other gran gave Mam her most evil stare: tiny green flints of venom.

We didn't know it then that upstairs, in bed, the living grandad was dead. My gran, not the other gran, came down and said he was one lazy soul. She'd been poking him in the ribs the whole night to fetch her a hot-water bottle and he'd thoroughly ignored her. The doc went up, and a few minutes later he stepped into the living room and said that the poor soul was dead as dead can be, already turning blue the way a dead lizard does in the sun. We could see why someone would pop a pistol at him.

The two grans grew close after that, and when they mixed each other's false teeth up, there wasn't as much as a cross word aired. They were coming out with their own secrets, slipping off their tongues on a slide of alcohol. Stuff I didn't want to hear, stuff that made me glad for Billy that he was deaf. They cried over their husbands – giving out shit about them but crying at the same time, and that struck me as being weird. Hating yet loving someone at the same time. I guess they were crying at life in general.

Billy and I played a lot together that summer. I felt really sorry for him. His hearing – it was bit like being given a present and then having it snatched away from you. He couldn't hear people calling his name on the baseball field. He'd sit bemused when we broke up laughing at *Bilko* re-runs on TV. He'd sit and watch and then go to our bedroom.

He lost the head once. Berserking our room and killing my goldfish in the process. Dad finally calmed him down. Mam wanted to flay his butt and Dad got really mad at her. His face turned crimson, and then white, and he let out a roar that shook us all to the core. He kicked the door closed in her face. Mam shook so much with fright she had to grip the banister for support. I went in later on, to check on things. Billy was sitting in Dad's lap, sobbing. I knew Dad had been crying too, because he kept looking through the window at the mountains. He combed Billy's hair with his fingers. I wondered then that maybe there was more wrong with

Billy than people were letting on. Later I asked Dad, and after he shook his head he said, 'No, son, I was thinking how Billy ain't going to hear nothing no more – not the birds singing, the leaves rustling, nor his kids calling his name.'

Mam said that although she was against the idea she would agree to let Billy attend special school. There's something persuasive about a quiet man losing his temper, I guess.

Billy taught me sign language and it's not so hard when you get used to it. The night Jethro Morphy went crazy and shot his whole family dead in their beds, Billy was teaching me his finger language. I jumped with fright at the rifle reports but Billy sat there, unafraid, unknowing.

We moved on when the grans died; they popped off within weeks of each other, taking each other's molars to the grave. Dad found something in Grandad's cigar box. A will. One that should have been read three years before. Seems like the other gran forgot about it, or maybe she thought it was a big joke. But when Dad checked things out – well, he was left a hundred thousand dollars between savings and insurance polices and a near-derelict hunting lodge near a lake. Dad figured the old guy was saving for a rainy day while he was getting wet all the time, only he didn't know it. The lodge was where he and Camel Delahunty used to rendezvous whenever she was in his neck of the woods.

We moved to a town near Billy's school. Dad got a job he liked and is fixing up the lodge so we can holiday there. Mam got another baby. A bolt from the blue, she said. All of us are hoping that he doesn't go deaf.

You See It So Clearly

Imagine a red sunset, a barbecue's smoky scent on the wane and a soft muggy stillness as darkness begins to pinch. Imagine the black crust of the skies finally sealing the reds and ambers. Stars begin to show and you're sitting there with your last beer when your wife joins you at the white plastic table in the garden. A garden you'd fashioned together – Amy believes that the couple who do things together stay together.

She sits across from you, her white plastic chair unbalancing, drawing an 'Oh Jesus!' from her as she quickly corrects herself by gripping the table rim. You ask if she's all right, even though it's obvious she is. You say it for the sake of saying something. That's how it is with you of late, saying things just to cross the silence that sometimes lies between you.

The kids are in the sitting room watching a DVD. Not your kids. Sophie's. Amy wants another of her own but she can't carry a child to term. Often she complains about the fact. You don't. One son is enough. One dead son is enough. Adam was lost in a car accident three

33

years ago, when he was eleven; his grandfather, Amy's father, who was driving, died with him.

She says the barbecue went well and you agree that it did and squeeze your beer can. And she looks at you in that searching way she has and realises that while you want to talk about it, you don't know how or where to start.

She asks what's on your mind. Amy can always tell when something is wrong. She smiles a come-out-with-it smile. Unburden yourself.

You think the smile has no natural home and yet understand that your own is also an orphan.

'Nothing, nothing,' you lie. You would prefer to be honest. You are into openness.

Imagine her sister comes out and joins you, her chair remaining steady, and lights a cigarette and leans forward and runs her hand down her leg and says she needs to shave.

Feigning crossness, your wife tells her sister to make herself decent. Sophie wears a low-cut top and a red miniskirt. She tugs on the mini, displaying out-of-character modesty and shyness.

You say nothing. Less than an hour ago your sister-in-law followed you into the upstairs bathroom and turned the key behind her and you kissed her and she kissed you and when your wife called from the bottom of the stairs and asked her where you'd got to, you both smiled and drank in the beer on each other's breath. She shouted out that she hadn't seen you. She whispered let's do it and you did, urgently and frantically without noise, silently gagging each other's sighs and moans into your shoulders and arms and necks. Shuddering to a grand finale accompanied by the chorus of a rapping noise on the door and one of her boys, Luke, saying he was bursting.

She said half-breathlessly, 'In a minute, Luke – for God's sake.'

And your wife called from downstairs, 'Sophie, are you OK?'

She said, eyes widening, your wife's eye colouring and shape, blue, round and younger, 'Fine – I'll be out in a sec.'

Then your wife said to Luke, 'Leave your mum alone for a few minutes – I think the downstairs bathroom is free now, hurry.'

She walked over to the toilet, rubbing herself with her knickers, mopping you up, and anchored her arse above the seat with the dolphin motifs, like a jockey raised above the saddle, and peed. She washed her hands, took the towel you'd proffered and fixed herself in her red miniskirt. You splashed some cold water on your face to dampen your bright colour.

'Jesus,' you said.

She whispered, 'That was nice.'

Nice.

You knew what made it nice for her was the fact that she'd stolen you from her sister, had done it under her sister's roof with nothing, only door space, between you and her. She did it because her sister has the big dormer with the big husband earning a big wage with a big car out front, while all she has is a mid-terrace house and a job in a store that she pretends to love. And a husband who doesn't love her and who divides his time amongst her, his children and his lover.

Sophie looks well, very well. Size-12 figure, decent breasts, long black hair, high cheekbones and good teeth.

The sisters are talking about a woman friend of theirs who adopted her sister's baby. You feel left out of the conversation and think about leaving them alone.

Sophie says the temperature's dropped. You say the gas has run out in the outdoor heater but it hasn't. You just think it'll do her no harm to feel the cold. You are being cruel and you dislike yourself for it.

She shawls her navy cardigan over her thin shoulders, crosses those long legs that had wrapped themselves around the backs of your knees, puffs on her Silk Cut Light. Looks at you and asks if there are any pepper steaks left. You squeeze your beer can, again. Your wife looks hard at you and says Sophie had spoken to you. You say sorry: you were distracted.

'A burger?' you suggest.

Sophie says, 'No – I have this terrific longing for a steak. I need to build myself up.'

Amy smiles. 'Sorry – sausages. Would sausages do?'

'I'm sick of eating sausage,' your Sophie says.

'I could do with a beer,' you say, aware of the word

sausage and Sophie's throw of her daring eyes at you as she breathed it.

Your wife says you've had enough to drink, that you could do with cutting back on the booze, could shed a few pounds too. She asks her sister what she thinks.

'Well, I prefer men with a bit of flesh on them.'

'Like Anthony?'

Her husband.

'Not like him, no. I said with a bit of flesh, not a ton of it.' She says this looking at you and adds that you're not obese.

Amy says it's gone too cold for her, and when she's indoors neither you nor her sister speak. Like kids sulking after rowing with each other.

Eventually she sighs and says, 'It's OK.'

'I—'

'It's OK.'

'It's far from OK.'

'Keeping it in the family, Dessie – where's the harm in that?' Sophie says, looking at her painted toenails looking up at her.

'She'll be hurt.'

'She won't.'

'She will, if she finds out.'

'It's been threatening to happen for a long time – I've seen you looking at me. The chemistry was right.' She does this thing from the *Pulp Fiction* movie –V signs her eyes – and says she can do *Grease*, sings softly, 'It's electrifying.'

You smooth your hair. Amy is going to pick and pick at your bones until she arrives at the truth. Sophie can handle stuff, bad stuff that doesn't show on her face. How often have you heard about shit going on in her home, and yet outdoors she'd wear a smile better than the happiest would manage?

Lots.

Sophie touches your toes with hers and says you've to cheer up. You wonder how she can remain so blasé about cheating on her sister. You ask.

She shrugs and says when you were both kids you used to swap clothes with and without each other's permission. 'This is more serious than swapping clothes.'

'You wanted the cake and you ate it – well, Dessie, sorry for you – but you can't cough it back up. Stop being stupid, will you?' She stares at you in a way that makes you feel your stupidity is a heavy load for her to bear.

You say it's getting chilly and cross the garden to the patio door and step into the kitchen. Amy is preparing supper. Luke comes in and asks for his mum and you say she's on her way in. He runs back into the sitting room.

Sophie's outside smoking a cigarette. You see the fullness of its strawberry light in your reflection in the patio glass, lending you a third eye in your forehead.

Amy asks you to call Sophie for her supper. When you don't, she pucks you gently in the arm and says you've to have your hearing tested and slides back the door and calls her younger sister.

It kills you at the maple table to see them talking over tomato-and-cheese sandwiches as though they are the best of friends. This disturbs you greatly. You could understand what had taken place a little better if there were a degree of animosity between them.

You wonder then if you were correct in your earlier appraisal of Sophie's motivation. Perhaps she isn't resentful of all her sister has going for her. Perhaps she genuinely fancies you. Hadn't Amy once found you irresistible? Sophie was right – you used to steal looks at her. You used to think of how it would be with her. The stolen looks did not go unnoticed and now you know how it is.

Sophie carries the boys' suppers on a tray to the sitting room.

'What's your problem with Sophie?' Amy says.

'I've no problem.'

'You've hardly spoken two words to her all evening – don't spoil staying here for her.'

You want to say something but she gets there first. 'You don't realise how difficult it was for me to persuade her to stay over for a few nights.'

'A few nights,' you say. This is news to you.

'Four or five – she doesn't want to be there when Anthony comes to collect his stuff.'

'So, she finally threw him out.'

'Too right – he was using the home as a halfway house. She gave him an ultimatum. He can't just wander back in whenever he wants. It's terrible to see those kids being upset – the rows that go on there. Listening to that couldn't be good for them. If I had kids …'

You grieve at the pain in Amy's face and glance at the framed photograph on the mantelpiece, too far away to be distinct. From a distance – the distance burns.

In bed, the middle of the night, some minutes after you'd turned off your lamp, you stare into the darkness.

Sophie's kids are in a deep sleep, worn out by their early-morning start, the long day spent at play, a longer evening spent in front of the television.

Sophie isn't asleep. You hear the weight of her feet on the landing, hear her look in on her two boys and shut their door. You do not hear her close her own.

You shut your eyes and roll onto your side. But you are unable to lose yourself. Amy's fingernails are on your neck, scratching ever so lightly.

Her hand falls away. You are sure she has surrendered to sleep. You wish you could do the same.

When Amy finds out she will be incredibly hurt. And she will find out. You have never cheated on her before, leastways not physically. Your eyes allied with your imagination have fornicated with many women – their identities locked in your mind, known only by your right hand. But you have convinced yourself that this is not cheating. In the strictest sense this is true.

Of all the women in all of the world you had to do it with her sister.

You feel Amy's hand on your back, pushing. Urging you.

'What?' you say, on edge.

'Go on.'

The push is stronger.

Of a sudden you see it all so clearly …

Old Ground

He has not been asleep for long. It's still dark, still raining and still the wind blows like a ceaseless soft sighing. The start of a wet and miserable Lebanese winter: hard rains, skies torn by jagged lightning, the booming angels at war, the cold and damp, the reeking smell from kerosene heaters, the failings in tin roofs that allow the rain to drip through.

He turns on a bedside lamp and eases from bed and dresses. The jacks are just beyond the mess and the concrete bunker. He slips into his parka and sandals and lowers himself to the heater. Wants to leak, but needs heat – the cold had woken him. Should have kept the heater going.

Taking it outside, he sets a match to its wick, hopeful that by the time he returns the soot on the wire globe will have been burned off. The Lebanese coldness reminds him of childhood mornings when the range's grate stank of ashes and all they had left to burn were a few furze sticks that had been gathered the previous evening.

He pisses into an urinal carrying strings of curled pubic hair and afterwards washes his hands thoroughly, using the last sheaves of a paper roll by the door to dry off. On his way he had seen the lights on in the mess, heard the strumming of a guitar. Three a.m. on Saturday morning, lightning on the horizon, distant peels of thunder. The rain spits now instead of torrential drops.

He steps this way – then that – in order to avoid puddles, and trips on a tree root that in time will break through the tarmac veiling it. 'There was an oul woman who lived …' sounds in the mess – where a crash of empty beer tins that the lads like to rise in pyramid formation on the low table is met by a mighty cheer. The song sentences along, the singer braving the storm, a lone oarsman on the back of waves.

He doesn't drink, never did, never will. They don't understand his loathing of alcohol. He tells them he hates its stink, the eejits it makes of people. The lads say he should lighten up. Have a drink – relax. Now, knowing his resistance is strong, they seldom offer to buy him a drink, instead leave a Sprite or a Coke in front of him, pitying him for not being able to leave himself behind.

If an alcoholic mother doesn't turn you off drinking then nothing will; she made several attempts to quit – six weeks the longest period of abstention. She was never a happy person. He always felt she had an itch to be away from the drudgery of rearing kids, and he later came to believe, without knowing for sure, that something from her past had haunted her all the way to the grave. He is like her in that he doesn't talk – he lets the lads wonder about the reasons behind his Pioneer status. His father says that her boozing drove him away – of course he would say that to soften his guilt.

The lads will sleep it off tomorrow, the long Saturday broken in two, while he will breakfast early and make for the border, walking the ten kilometres to Nahariya to spend some time on the streets. Drink coffee and eat a falafel lunch in Sanso's – all depends on the weather – bloody weather, it can make a prisoner of your plans. If worse comes to worse, he will jog a while in the Rubb Hall and give his room a good cleaning – the right time for it when his two room-mates are away on leave.

The heater's wire globe is beginning to redden as he lifts its chrome handle and enters his billet. Setting the heater close to his bed he rubs his eyes and begins to undress.

'Who is it?' slurs a woman's voice.

With a start his jeans choke his ankles and he stumbles over.

'Jesus, Mary …' he says, getting to his feet and bringing up his jeans, fingers feeling for buttons.

He squints hard into the darkened corner, then hits the main fluorescent switch. Blink … buzzing … blink … then a constant light, a constant humming.

She is about thirty with long auburn hair and a face that he would have classed as beautiful, were it not for

44

the film of dark hair above her lip. She lies naked under a thin white sheet. He glances away. She is drunk. Her hair is damp. The smell from her – he hasn't smelt drink so strong from a woman in some time. His eyes turn to his beach towel draped across his chair. Used.

'What the – who are you?'

She sways on the bed as if his question has rocked her. 'Tina … I am Tina.'

Slavic accent – a Polish nurse from the UN hospital? If so, he hasn't seen her before.

She tries to get to her feet but flops back down. Hiccups. Sits up.

'He will kill me,' she says.

'Who? Who will kill you?'

'Peter.'

'Who is Peter?'

'My husband.'

Small belches escape her.

What to do? She rocks herself forward and back, sings in a low voice, in Polish, 'All Kinds of Everything'. He tells her to stop – there are people trying to sleep next door. She stops – asks if she can sleep here tonight – please?

'No – your husband.'

'Is with someone else.' Laughs. 'I suppose it is me who should kill him, yes?'

Tears roll along her cheeks. She dabs at them with the back of her wrist and doesn't know that the sheet has fallen from her shoulders. Tina is slim and bronzed.

Stretch marks girdle her waist. She looks at him. Green eyes – large and round – misty. She gathers the sheet about herself with no urgency.

She tilts her head, her eyebrows joining in a puzzled frown.

'Norwegian?'

'Irish.'

'Oh … Irish. Peter has a good friend who is Irish.'

He is aware of his incipient pot belly under her surmising eye, his age, the wrinkles about his eyes, the thinning hair that shows silver and copper at the temples. His eyes, one slightly smaller than the other, both as grey as washed stone.

'Where are your clothes?'

'In the sea.'

'In the sea?'

'Yes. The sea – I put them there.'

The shore is a hundred yards away. Quiet slips of wave to seashore drowned out by the thunder and hard rain. Down the steps behind the mess – but the gate leading to the beach is locked by the French guard every evening, promptly at six. She says Peter has a key. 'Have you a drink in your room? Your name – what is your name?'

'Myles – and no, I don't have anything to drink – except a fruit juice – in the fridge.'

'I need to piss.'

She gets to her feet on the second attempt, pads barefooted outside and squats by the prefab not entirely out of his view. He assumed she had been heading for the camp toilets. Hearing the soft shush, her series of hiccups, he looks away. She makes a noisy entrance, the door slamming behind her like a Venus flytrap – a pair in a situation. She resembles an Indian squaw wearing that blooming sheet. Standing in front of the fire, she says, 'Please let me stay.'

He looks at his watch. Kind of dangerous this – alone with a strange woman – what if she makes allegations against him tomorrow? You hear of such things happening. But it is so late.

'I promise – no trouble. I just do not want to go back to my room, tonight – I am afraid.'

'Of Peter?'

'Of me.'

He breathes, 'OK, fine, right ...'

She smiles, moves from the heater and makes for the bed, crawling in under a grey blanket he had spread for her.

He watches her for moments. Her hair lies in loose strands across her face, eyes closed – she is sinking towards sleep. He breaks for his bed and hits the light. He thinks he should head for another billet but the only available accommodation is a damp cell in the Duty Room. Sleep overtakes him before the kerosene can run out and the coldness set in to keep him awake.

It is a shallow sleep and doesn't last for long. He studies the small luminous crucifix he had nailed to a strip of chipboard above the window. The red shadowy light cast by the heater has begun to fade.

The smell of drink – God – is she awake? She isn't snoring.

Silence. The room is almost perfectly silent. She could be dead. No! No way. Choked on her vomit – a familiar old fear that has not put a tremor in his soul for years.

He clambers from bed, turns on his bedside light and dresses in shorts and a fresh T-shirt. Rubs the sleep from his eyes. The morning coldness cuts in, so he takes out the single-bar heater from under his bed – it's against regulations to use them because of the draw on the generators – but it's only for an hour, to take the chill from the air. Roots out an old tracksuit and new, cheap quality flip-flops from his locker. Fastens the Velcro straps on his own sandals.

He looks in at the corner, distinguishes her bulk in the grey light filtering in through the window. A silent sleeper. Opening the fridge door he takes out a bottle of water and fills the small quick-to-boil plastic kettle he had bought from a street trader. Shares out the last grains from a coffee jar into two cups. Calls her. No response. He makes the coffee black and sugary.

'Here,' he says, rocking her shoulder gently, turning on her light.

Smell of stale alcohol. How often had he done the same with his mother, waking her with a cup of strong tea? Countless times and then a last time – always the same smell from her.

Tina opens her eyes. Closes them, opens again. Remembers. Takes in the coffee.

'It's time for you to go,' he says, 'you can wear an old tracksuit of mine. It's clean.'

She nods. He leaves the tracksuit and flip-flops on the bed and turns from her to drink his coffee and watch the sun begin to rise from behind distant hills, showing through dropped stitches in the clouds. She slurps on her coffee and, dressing quickly, joins him at the fire, her teeth chattering, hands surrounding her cup for the heat. He notices her wedding band. She is shorter than he is and thinner than he had first thought. She is close to him, almost touching. He doesn't move away and she doesn't inch any closer. The muezzin crier kicks in.

'Thank you,' she says.

'It's OK.'

'I do not usually get so drunk … Last night was different. I did not want to see another day.'

He faces her, frowns.

'I could not do it – just could not follow my clothes into the sea – it started to rain, lots of rain. I turned back.' She smiles at herself – then shrugs. 'You must think I am crazy.'

He puts his hand on her shoulder and squeezes. Sips the last of his coffee. She tells him she had come over to surprise her husband for his fortieth birthday. He is a major in the Engineers. And she did surprise him – him and his lover. How could he – how could he do this to her?

When she has composed herself, he accompanies her to the main gates. She says she knows the way. He offers a lift because it's a long walk but she shakes her head and says she needs the air.

He gets ready for his walk to Nahariya.

Thinks of her. Thinks of his mother, too.

He wonders which way Tina will choose. And knows before he hits the bend in the road, knows from what, experience? Yes – and from that feeling he sometimes gets when he is walking in a strange place, yet knows it's old ground.

Bone Deep

They found a woman's skeleton in a well at the Market Square. The well had been covered by a grey boulder I used to sit on while waiting for a CIÉ bus to turn the corner at the traffic lights. The council had moved in with bulldozers and donkey-jacketed men to put a new face with new EU money on an old landmark. But for that reason the skeleton would not have been discovered.

An expert suggested the skeleton was over a hundred years old, if not more. Experts never give precise answers to anything. They hedge their bets and in that way can never be totally wrong – never being wrong is extremely important to a lot of people. Especially experts. My father is an expert.

He said the skeleton probably fell in during the rising of 1798. She might have been thrown into the well, and left there to drown. My father is tipsy. It is ten-past-nine on Sunday evening. He has been tipsy all day. He gets like this once a week.

We are in the sitting room at the American oak table Mum's father left us. Its stout legs are riddled with woodworm. Earlier, Dad made ham and mustard sandwiches. None of us eat them; we don't like the thick fat he leaves hanging like curtain frills over the crusts.

Ann is my youngest sister. Elly is the oldest; she is pregnant again but married this time. She did one before she did the other. Dad does not know. He thinks his grandson was born prematurely. Terry is the twin who survived the car accident. He is sixteen, three years older than me. He cannot talk, nor move from the waist down. His blue eyes are clouded, and when he tries to speak we make excuses to leave. He does not make pretty sounds.

Mum is at bingo. She never wins. It is her night out. She doesn't like leaving Terry and we don't like her leaving him either. His twin, Marcus, is with us in framed photographs on the mantelpiece.

'So, the skeleton didn't make the news, eh?' Dad says.

He's a short round man with thick hairy forearms. His fair hair is coarse and badly cut. It is badly cut because he insists on going to Oscar Henry the poor-sighted barber on the main street, beside the Castle Inn. Dad goes to him because he never has to queue. He does not stop to think why.

After the accident Mum and Dad didn't speak to each other for a long time. Marcus was dead and Terry was clinging to life in a hospital ward. He was in a lot of pain. Elly, Ann and me didn't go on the drive with Dad. If we had, I am sure one, two or all of us would have been killed.

A week after Marcus was buried Dad arrived home from hospital and told us all to pray for Holy God to take Terry – our brother was suffering too much. We started to cry and he changed his mind and said we'd to pray for him to live.

Ann and I look at each other. She wipes Terry's mouth. He can't keep the Rolos Dad bought for him in his mouth. He loves Rolos. Most of the chocolate he gets on his chin and shirt. Terry has to wear a white shirt; he will not wear a shirt of any other colour. We don't know why this is so.

Ann wipes Terry's mouth again. She will do this a number of times. On each occasion she will scowl at Dad. She has told me that Terry is Dad's mistake, and that he should be the one to clean his chin.

'Did you see the skeleton, Ian?' Dad says.

'No. I couldn't get close enough because of the crowd,' I say.

'I did. I'd say she was a young woman. She was very small. The archaeologist reckons she was fifteen or thereabouts.'

He is talking to me because Ann won't talk to him. She talks to him as little as possible.

'How do you think the skeleton got there?' he asks.

I shrug. I do not know, nor care. It has nothing to do with me. Dad works as a machine operator in a factory on the outskirts of town. He has lost the small finger of his left hand to a press. If he concentrated on his job and didn't drift off to places and matters not of his concern, he would not be a finger short. Perhaps he would not be a son and a half-of-a-son short, either.

His big round face expects an answer.

'Was the skeleton a skeleton before it ended up in the well?' I ask.

He nods, says, 'No.'

I try to sound like the expert I'd overheard and say, 'I think the woman got drunk and fell into the well. She was hidden from view by the water. The well was, of course, poisoned by her decaying corpse, and thus sealed.'

'That's very good. Very good.'

He looks at me with fresh respect. He is happy to be sending me to a private college. He says I'll do fine – I have his brains. I would like to say carrying his brains through college isn't a burden, the weight of a flea on a dog's back.

He sips at his beer. Sniffles. Sometimes he looks at Terry and an inner hurting digs deep creases about his eyes. He fell asleep behind the wheel.

'I wonder what colour hair she had,' Ann says.

'Dark haired,' Dad nods, 'I'd say dark hair … the odds are good that it was dark.'

'If she were pretty?' Ann continues.

Dad is under the impression that Ann is asking him, while in fact her questions aren't aimed at anyone in particular. She is more thinking aloud than anything.

'Yes, very pretty, the angle of her jawline, her teeth straight and all present, the slope of her skull, yes, she was pretty. But then who really knows?'

If I had seen the skeleton I wouldn't have tried to fit a face and a body to its bones. Instead, I'd have imagined myself as a skeleton and I would have found that an alarming and intriguing prospect. I would tell myself that I could not distinguish one skeleton from another, and that it appears we all end up looking the same.

'Did they find clothes?' Ann says.

'God, aye, they did,' Dad says.

'What exactly?' Ann is interested in clothes. She hopes to be a fashion designer.

'Black stuff.'

'Shawl, dress, skirt, what?'

Dad glances at me and shrugs, 'I don't know – they were in a Dunnes Stores bag.'

He laughs. His cheeks shudder when he laughs.

A spasm of displeasure crosses Ann's face. 'I'd say she was murdered.'

'Murdered. What makes you think that?' Dad says.

I would like to leave because I sense Ann is going to cut at Dad. She will cut him once too often.

'Look at all the women being murdered today – men are just animals. Animals then, and animals now.'

'Animals,' Dad muses.

One day I am sure he will draw her out. There will be a row and Ann will go to live with Elly. Then on bingo nights Dad will sit alone with Terry and wipe his chin free of chocolate.

Dad takes her in, runs a hand over his hair and

pinches the grey at his temple. Ann ignores him and hands Terry the TV remote.

I ask him a question to divert his suspicion. I do this because I don't want a spat in the house, and to stop Terry trying to shut up the row with his half-tongue.

'What will happen to the skeleton now, Dad?'

He likes it when his opinion is sought; it makes him feel important. He likes to feel important. He does not realise that in eyes not necessarily mine he has long ceased to be important. He is seen as the thorn in Daniel's lion, the ice that tore the *Titanic*, the driver who killed a brother, left another badly broken and crushed a mother's soul.

'They'll bring it to the – '

'The Zoo ...' Ann says, 'for animals to lick the bones.'

Silence, apart from the TV, where Jerry the Mouse is tormenting Tom the Cat. The cartoon pair never talk. This sits well with Terry.

Dad's lips open and close but his words don't arrive. The beer can at his elbow is empty. The fridge is out of beer.

Finally, he says, 'You're breathing the word "animal" a lot tonight – are you in double-speak mode?'

Ann's cheeks redden. She has a triangular face with pretty pursed lips you'd think were always poised to kiss.

'I'm sick of it!' she snaps, throwing Terry's chocolate-smattered tissue at Dad.

It is too late to stop the argument. The only hope is

for Ann to bolt for the door. He may or may not follow her. He won't if I tell him she's been acting funny all day. Then he will put her mood down to woman trouble, and make an allowance for her. He will shout up the stairs after her and tell her how lucky she is to be a woman. I take it that if I spoke to him in Ann's way I wouldn't be so fortunate.

What's happened before doesn't happen now. Ann doesn't leave. She is so sick of everything she wants to fight. 'I think all men are animals. Drunken, lousy drivers of animals.'

The tension has gotten deeper and darker. TV Tom is bent over a mouse hole, fingers in his ears, waiting for the bang from a red stick of dynamite which he does not know Jerry has moved behind him. I try to focus on the cartoon and point for Terry to do likewise, but he is looking at Dad and Ann. I wish they'd notice the change in him.

Dad's hands come together and his eyes fill with tears. All his rising anger has suddenly dissipated. Ann averts her glare, proffers the Rolos to Terry, but he sweeps them from her and they land with a soft plop on the fireside rug. She goes to wipe his chin but he angles his head away from her. My brother is chalk-faced. He should have braces on his teeth because of a bad over-bite, but his teeth have begun to fall out; the dentist says the roots were badly shaken in the crash.

His wet eyes are on Dad's. He tries to talk. It is an awful sound to listen to. A half-tongue flapping in a broken head. Ann sighs. She thinks he is being difficult because of the row that was shaping up but has blown over. In fact she is quite wrong. I am no expert, but I think it's because he has forgiven Dad for the crash, and is annoyed because the rest of us haven't. He can read the hurt, the remorse in Dad. While we want to punish, he doesn't.

Ann leaves the room in a huff. And I follow. I just can't listen to Terry going on and on in a tongue that sounds his torture. But I realise we want to escape from more than Dad and Terry. It is our shame at not being able to do what Terry has done. The accident may have taken much from him, but it hasn't taken everything.

He and Dad are alone. I put my ear to the door.

I hear Dad say to Terry that he has another packet of sweets. Not to worry. There's not so much as a peep from my brother.

Sometimes we forget how close they are.

Bone deep.

Black George

He came from the hills of Antrim and spoke in a thick Northern Ireland accent from the corner of his mouth, as if everything he said was confidential, a secret he was parting with for your ears alone.

He wore suits, always dark like spoiled clouds, and they were never without creases. He was taller than Dad; then again, as Black George said, everyone with legs under his arse stood taller than Dad.

We'd waken on Friday mornings to find Black George sitting at our table chasing a rasher around the plate. His red-apple cheeks freshly washed and shaved, his teeth in, his dark eyes like washed lumps of coal, he'd say, 'Morning, men.'

He'd lick his fingers after eating and Mum would be standing over the frying pan, her lips tight. She refused to reprimand Dad's friend, reprimanded us instead. And we knew better than to say we weren't licking our fingers.

Dad brought home lots of friends during the racing season. He'd meet them at the races or in the Stand

House Pub across the road from the track. Mum said every hungry stray in the place followed him home. Those were the days when money was tight and Mam and Dad got along.

Once he brought home a German doctor and his wife who smoked rolled-up cigarettes that stank of something like bad feet. They sang 'Silent Night' in German a couple of times. Mum didn't like the woman, the way her short skirt gave little peeps of her pink underwear. Dad never complained, nor did Black George who nudged Mum every time the skirt climbed a fraction, as if he believed that Mum too took a pleasure in the sight. Dad also brought home a Canadian jockey called Hagan. He'd red hair and a face primed to cry, his lips almost absent, turned inwards, as if kissing the hurting that was going on inside.

Black George loved the Curragh. He said the scent of furze was like an air freshener in his lungs. Dad'd nod when he'd say things like that. They never spoke about politics. Not even when things got rough in the North and Black George drew strange looks in the Railway Arms Hotel. On Sunday evenings a man with a kind face but hard eyes would drop a banned Republican pamphlet on the tables and wait for a small donation to land in his palm. Most fed him something, no matter how small, just to be rid of him. This particular Sunday Dad brought Black George into the hotel, forgetting about the Sunday caller. When he lighted at their table Black George fell silent and stared into his drink.

Dad's smile, his ready quips, defused the situation; he never brought Black George back there.

That's the story Dad spun Mum when Black George missed a couple of race meetings. He'd ring to say something had come up, and Dad would nod, give an understanding sigh because he liked the big man and say OK. Later he was to discover that Black George's absences had more to do with wife trouble than any residual feeling of fear or intimidation.

Meanwhile Dad continued to attend race meetings. He did well out of gambling, much better than he did as a jockey; it was as if his happy-go-lucky disposition was admired by the gods. But he'd never admit to being either lucky or unlucky. Luck had a role but not a significant one, he'd say, after hours spent studying the form, and weeding sense from the hundreds of horse whispers that flooded town on race day. Luck? You made your own.

People in town were always giving tips: this is a fucken certainty; a sure thing; flying it is; shit-hot; come home on its own. Dad had an uncanny knack of knowing what a horse was capable of. But a run of bad luck, while only diminishing his smile, forced him into accepting a foreman's position in a stable of crocks and no-hopers. Looking on the bright side, he told Black George over the phone that he needed a source of inside information.

Black George owned a factory somewhere up North, outside Newry. He'd arrive in with trays of unwrapped chocolate bars and tell us to get stuck in, ignoring Mum's saying we hadn't eaten dinner. When he recommenced visiting with the chocolates, Mum smiled and asked him how he was keeping.

Black George's beetle-black eyebrows gave a small lift. 'I'm sound as a trout.'

'Margie?' Mum said.

He shook his head and looked at the table as though it were gone-off chocolate and said, 'She's gone home to Malta. She didn't like the bombs going off and people being shot dead. It did her head in.'

According to Dad, Margie wouldn't have settled even if things in the North were quiet. She didn't appear to be interested in meeting people; the sort no sooner sitting down than she wanted to be on the move again.

When Black George was absent from the racing scene, Dad sometimes brought home another friend. A vet. This man wore thick lenses in his glasses. Liam was short and chubby-faced, and like Black George he wore suits, except his were lighter in colour. He'd a deep voice and vivid green eyes.

After a few drinks he liked to sing; Michael rowed the boat ashore and another about a train always being late, his two favourites. He sang other songs, too. Rebel ballads about Pearse and Connolly. Songs Dad knew but sang half-heartedly because he didn't like guns and bullets; maintained that killing or dying by them was nothing to sing about. He said so to Liam and the vet rubbed his balding head and nodded, in understanding, not in agreement.

Black George told Dad he wanted to buy a racehorse. Dad asked if he would be interested in buying into a partnership with a friend of his who'd just bought a grey colt. Black George hesitated. He'd lost a little weight, which Mum said proved how lost he was without Margie his wife. Dad said he'd given up eating his own chocolate bars. Black George smiled at what Mam and Dad said. It was a worried little smile that painted a picture for Dad – of how his friend's mind ached.

Black George liked the horse if not Liam. Dad was later to say the partnership had been a bad idea from the start. Liam was a true Green Republican and Black George a true Orange Loyalist. Incompatible colours. When Dad was tipsy he berated them both; saying the horse wouldn't be called Rebel Pride or Orange Might but All Friends.

The horse won three races but neither Black George nor Liam – Mum called him Green Liam – ever stood in the parade ring together. And the partnership was broken up after a row at home when Liam said something in Irish and got a shock when Black George twigged and told him quietly but fiercely that there were a million guns up North, all saying No!

Dad got vexed then with the pair and put Liam out, telling him to cool down and get sense. Then he rounded on Black George, not for what he had said but for rising to the bait and losing his cool. Black George, standing head and shoulders above Dad, shrugged and spread his hands in embarrassment.

Liam phoned afterwards and said he was sorry, that it had been drink talk and how was he to know that Black George had any Irish?

The flat season ended as winter set in, and we didn't see much of Black George. He sent a card for Christmas and a box of wrapped-up chocolates. He'd ring Dad now and then, and Dad would always return the calls.

Early in the New Year Black George rang to say he was going to Leopardstown. Dad said he would go if he could bring Liam. Black George went silent and then uttered the 'Yes' that likely saved his life.

It was in a pub after the races that it happened. A man followed Dad and Black George into the toilets. A pistol was produced against Black George's neck. Dad went outside and got Liam. Later on, with Black George trembling like a leaf about to be wind-blown, Liam apologised, 'Mistaken identity ...'

Dad told Mum all this with disgust etched in his face. But that episode was lost amongst the other things that happened in and around the same time. Mum and Dad weren't getting along. Arguments broke out over ridiculous things. They no longer shared the same bedroom, and when I walked into the kitchen one morning, ready with the news that I was taking Dad's advice and heading to New York, the atmosphere was charged.

It took a short while to find out why. Mum suspected Dad of having an affair with a younger, much younger, woman. I didn't know the truth of it. But a couple of months after I'd left for America, Dad rang to say he'd moved down the country. Mum called the same evening. She put a brave voice on things and insisted he'd be back when he'd thought matters through.

Mum liked to write to me, but Dad preferred to phone. He kept me informed about Black George. Told me that Black George's teenage daughter was killed by a hit-and-run driver in Valletta.

Dad attended the funeral. He said it was such a waste of young life. Apparently Black George stayed away at the funeral from Margie's people. According to Dad, he didn't reveal much outward emotion; eyes squinted, lips caught in a grimace. No tears, not a one.

Around the same time Green Liam found out that he had cancer and was given six months. He refused to see anyone, even Dad. He has it in the face, Dad said.

I suspect Dad had met Phil in Newry. He was travelling up and down there a lot to see if he could help Black George. Seems the only time the big man opened up was when the two of them nursed a whiskey bottle the night through.

He'd cry sometimes and talk about his daughter. Margie his Maltese ex had come back into his life, but Black George had no interest in making a proper go of things.

Dad didn't tell me about Black George's whiskey tears or the Maltese ex. Black George himself told me when he visited me in Woodside on a freezing Christmas Eve. The two of us welcomed Christmas dawn with a bottle of Chivas Regal and thick Cuban cigars.

He admired the photographs of Dad I had on the wall. Dad and his chestnut dream-horse, the pair snapped mid-air over a Baldoyle fence. Black George had lost weight around the face and the red-apple flush was now a dangerous purple in his cheeks. He spoke in the low tones of a depressed man, the twinkle of humour clouded over in his eyes. He managed a smile when I reminded him of the time he inked over the Pope's eye in a newspaper photograph and of Green Liam singing 'Amhrán na bhFiann' after another row had passed, and he, 'God Save the Queen', the two of them langers, holding each other up and slurring the words of both songs.

Black George nodded, stared into his drink and told me Green Liam had died recently. Black George had business in New York, dismantling a business partnership that had something to do with Margie. The night before he left he treated me to a Chinese meal, where he mentioned Phil to me, about how much happier Dad was since meeting her.

He pressed a few notes into my hand, and wouldn't hear tell of me refusing. 'You're only getting on your feet, boy – sure there's no sense in it resting in my wallet when it could be doing you some good. You might want to visit home in the summer.'

I watched him leaving in a yellow cab. The money he'd given me was a decent sum. I remembered how he'd always had a decent streak in his bones; was always handing me, my sisters and brothers pocket money.

I heard he had bailed Green Liam out of trouble too. But he'd never admit to doing it, had told Dad it was a debt repaid.

Mum called shortly afterwards in near hysteria. Dad was living with someone down the country. The shame of it, she said. I asked her was the loss of him not worse than the shame and she said nothing.

I met Dad and Black George in the summer at a Curragh race meeting. The sky was blue and the gambled-on horse did not mar the good day. Black George was, if not back to himself, then as close to it as he'd been for a long time. Dad was relaxed and good humoured. He asked me to go see him riding in a vets' race in Tipperary, and I did.

On the day, Black George drove us to the racecourse. The horse finished third, and between Dad's youthful glow and Black George's burst of smiling, you'd think the pair of them had just performed a miracle or something.

Black George lent me his car to drop Dad home. He was heading up North on the train after staying overnight in a bed & breakfast. He'd company – that's why he didn't come with us. A blonde woman with freckles. Black George said she reminded him of the German doctor's wife.

I met Phil in Dad's cottage that evening and got along with her after a somewhat nervous start. Later that night, in Mum's, I had to tell her that Dad wouldn't be coming home. Not ever.

Black George said the blonde woman was a disappointment. If she'd pink underwear like the German
doctor's wife he never got to find out. Shortly afterwards he sold his business. A few months later he was
on about moving to Scotland and marrying a widow
he'd met through a dating agency. She was an artist, he
said, and a good one too. Dad thought he was joking
again, and didn't think anymore of it until the arrival of
a gilt-edged wedding invitation.

Dad rang to let me know how the occasion had
gone. Rain all day and a bitter bone-scraping wind. But
the weather didn't blunt the smiles on the faces of Black
George and his new wife, who Dad thought bore an
uncanny resemblance to Margie his Maltese ex.

Gloria, Black Gloria as Dad called her, was just what
his friend needed in his life. She'd a veneer of toughness
covering a kind heart.

But he was saddened to learn that Black George was
finished with Curragh race days – that Gloria had called
time on his carousing after the two of them went on a
rip some days back from his honeymoon.

I didn't hear anything of Black George then for four
or five years. Not until Phil rang and broke the news to
me about Dad. We met at the funeral.

My mother wasn't there, but Hagan the Canadian
jockey was, his lips no longer kissing his hurt. Red hair
slicked and polished but thinner than before. He'd a
new woman on his arm. He said Dad was there for him
when he needed a friend.

Black George was pale and shook looking. Gloria was very much in love with him. You could see that, the way she stood beside him, squeezing his hand.

Afterwards in a bar where I'd arranged refreshments, Black George nursed a large brandy, while Gloria and Phil were having a chat; Phil semi-listening as Gloria gently touched her arm.

Black George had tears in his eyes but they were gone in a couple of snuffles and a bite on his lower lip. He said if I needed anything to let him know. Said that my father was a sound man, a real friend. One who didn't mind getting his shoes wet for you. He put his hand on my shoulder and then walked away. He walked slowly, like his feet were in pain. I never saw him again.

A few years years later Gloria wrote, sent a large package. Her name took a moment to register with me. Her letter was short and to the point. Black George, she wrote, died on 4 February at home in Edinburgh after a brief illness. He'd wanted me to have something – a picture to hang on the wall with the others he'd seen on his visit to my apartment. A painting of three men. Known to me. They're standing in a parade ring, smiling, all holding cigars, next to a bay horse. The caption underneath in dark type reads: All Friends.

In Patsy's

At lunchtime I went into Patsy's and paid for a lasagne before I realised there weren't any available tables.

This woman I knew to see looked at me and said the chair across from her wasn't taken. She moved a side plate that had given me the impression the seat had been spoken for.

'That's camouflage – in case some fucker I don't like went to sit across from me.'

So I sat down. She wore a brown jacket with a blue scarf around her neck. Suddenly an image of her streaked across my mind: red shoes and redder mini-skirt. Years ago I'd been on duty in the public office of the military police and one night after things had quietened, around 4 a.m., I heard the quick and determined beat of a woman's high heels on the march. The buzzer sounded. I looked at her through the door's spy hole. She stood on the steps, wisps of snow blowing about her, flakes turning to spots of grey melt in her hair.

I let her in and she went immediately to the glow of an electric wall-heater. She asked me for tea and I brought her a cup which she wrapped her hands about like it were something she cherished – had lost and now found.

Breege? Yeah. Surname? Kennedy? That was her maiden name. Married? Fingers click in my brain. Got it. Foster. She'd aged and puffed out a little. She had a salad in front of her, a fork in her hand. But there was no appetite in her green eyes.

'How are you going?' She pushed a slice of potato about the plate.

'OK. Yourself?'

'Dying.'

I was looking about when she said this, trying to catch the eye of the girl at the cash register who'd said she'd have someone bring over my garlic bread.

'They're fuckers,' Breege said.

'All they want is your money,' she continued, 'and you out of here as fast as you can swallow. But fuck them; I'm staying here for as long I like.'

I concentrated on eating my lasagne. A lot of cheese and little meat, and the oval-shaped dish appeared to have shrunk since I was last here.

Breege wore gold rings on three of her fingers. Wrinkles ran like heavy tributaries from the corners of her eyes, and a frown had cut a permanent niche for itself in her forehead.

'Are you still in the army?'

'No. I'm out about three years.'

'And what are you at these days?'

'Bits and pieces. I write. I paint houses when the money's slow in coming for the writing, or I'm a security guard. Mostly I write – irrespective of what else I have to do.'

She said she'd read a story I'd written for some woman's magazine. It was good. She didn't like the ending though. A real woman wouldn't have taken her dying husband back, not after what he'd done, driving her son into committing suicide.

I said that was her way of punishing him.

The niche in her forehead grew deeper.

I said that every day he was at home for her to remind him, and crowd his head with memories, photos and such like, and subtly cut at him for the things he said and did to their boy.

'You didn't say that in your story.'

The reader had to suss that much out, I said. I'd sown enough clues in the form of interior monologue, but I said nothing of that to Breege. She shook her head and said she hoped I didn't leave the houses I painted half-finished, for my clients to guess at how the rest of the walls would look.

She didn't smile. And her tone was the same monotone as that dawn morning – what … six, five years ago?

'And where are you working, Breege?'

'I'm dying. So I've quit working. I used to waitress in a Chinese restaurant at night and in the mornings do the same on breakfast tables in a roadside café.'

'There's a bad dose going around – it's something to

do with the sudden drop in – '

'Not flu dying,' she cut across me. 'Really dying – take more than a Lemsip to save me. I need a fucking miracle.'

The garlic bread arrived, wrapped in tinfoil, brought by an Asian man who appeared to have no chin. He had a generous helping of brown eyes though.

'I'm sorry to hear that.'

'No. You're not. You don't care about me. You're just being polite. But I can tell I'm not dirt in your eyes, no low-life scum. Some people look at me like I was some-thing the cat did in its litter tray.'

'Ah now, Breege …'

'Ah now my hole. It's true.'

I was polite to her when she was in the office. She said she wanted her husband out of her house. She stood there with her arms folded and her legs crossed. He'd had another woman in her home, in her bed. A bed she'd saved for an age to buy – orthopaedic; for her back, don't you know – her lower spine was fucked.

'Ye sort it or I will – I'll stick a knife up his arse and then hers – whoever she is.'

If you want people to believe something, whisper it – and Breege's deadpan voice left me in no doubt that Dermot Foster had a blade waiting for him. It was why she had come to the duty room rather than go home. She knew her capacity for harm, was acutely, fearfully aware of it even if she was half-steamed.

I radioed the patrol and had them speak to Dermot and he volunteered to move into barracks for the night.

Dermot's next-door neighbour had been his bed guest. We didn't tell Breege. I've a sketchy memory of this, but I'm almost certain she found out a month or so later and she had used the blade she had, driving it into her sleeping husband's buttock in a drunken effort to castrate him from behind.

'Are you living in town here?' I asked.

'I am – I have a bedsit. Dermot's gone years, good riddance. He's in England now. The son, Jamesy, was in court this morning. That's where I've come from. He got Saint Pat's for six months. He's running with a bad crowd. He's the eejit the others get to do all the dirty, risky work.'

'How old is he?'

'Twenty-three.'

'A pity to see him –'

She waved her hand at me, then placed it on the table by her plate as though she'd snared a truth. 'Brains to burn. Buy and sell you at computers, he would. He's only to look at a computer to know what's not working in it.'

I'd heard this sort of thing from other women, all claiming their children had great talent, were returning to college to do this and that. Shite talk. Clinging to hope. Their kids were dysfunctional in some way or other – robbed, took drugs, boozed too hard, assaulted people. They didn't even make the grade as ordinary kids, and that killed something in their mothers.

The Asian wore a name badge called Charlie. He lifted my empty side plate and started for my coffee. I told him I wasn't finished with it.

'Fuck off,' Breege said to him.

He looked at her and then at me.

'We need the tables. People are waiting. I'm sorry.'

'Fuck off,' she said.

I asked Charlie for a refill of coffee. When he was gone, I said to Breege there were politer ways of telling someone to eff off. Socially acceptable methods.

'I'm speaking my everyday language,' she said.

In the time I was with her she must have pushed her food around the plate a dozen times. A hippodrome, the chariots corn, potato salad, pasta, ham pieces.

The fork had yet to reach her mouth.

'It's not him. It's those other fuckers – grab your money and kick you straight out they would – if they thought you'd an arse that'd sit still and allow it to happen. Not fucking me. Look at her, look at your woman there behind the register. The head dyed off her. Smug puss, nose in the air like we were pigs come to the trough. I'd love to slap her fucking face. If you could call it a face.'

I regretted having asked for the refill.

'How many kids have you got?' she asked.

'Three.'

'Boys?'

'Girls, all girls.'

'I've one daughter. She's living with that bastard

Dermot in London. Her real name is Bridie but he made her change it to Jenny. Bridie was my mother's name. And she was right about him. A conniving prick, she said. Right from the word go she had him sussed. I had to let Bridie go live with him – I didn't want her here when it's coming to the end. I wrote her a letter and Jamesy – and Dermot too. They won't be sent to them until I'm gone. Nice letters to my kids but I hope the ink jumps off the page into Dermot's eyes and blinds the fucker.'

'He was that bad? Really?'

She looked hard at me. Like people sometimes do when they assume without basis that you know everything about them – especially the dirt.

'Jaysus, you were in the miltary police – you must've known.'

'I spent a lot of time abroad.'

'He used to stub his cigarettes out on Jamesy.'

'Christ.'

'Beat me a couple of times to within an inch of my life.'

I saw that I was expected to listen and not comment.

'Pushed me on to other men.'

But what she said next almost caused me to fall from the chair.

'He won me in a game of poker you know?'

'What?'

'My brother Sammy bet me in a poker game and Dermot won me.'

'How old were you?'

'Eighteen. I didn't mind. I'd been won before, only the lads usually gave me back after they got their bit, but he didn't. He said he was hanging onto me and then we got married.'

'A card game,' I said, incredulously.

'Now isn't that a story for you to write?'

'It is.'

'And don't fucking go leaving it open at the end – tell people what happened. Exactly.'

'How did you feel when …?'

'Sure I didn't mind too much. Why should I? I enjoyed myself, I did. I was wild. Lived in a wild place in Athy, a wild house, where all this mad energy was stored up – we were a shit-poor family and drinking booze from the time we left the tit. And smoking anything we could get our hands on. Behind closed doors, isn't that right?'

I nodded and sighed.

'What do you think of that? You write it down. It'll be a bestseller. Write a real book and stop messing about with those stories that don't have proper endings.'

'Life doesn't have proper endings.'

'Mine does. When I'm dead it's over. That's a proper ending.'

'You really think so?'

'Oh don't gimme all that shit about heaven and hell and seeing the white light …'

Around us people milled, holding Formica trays.

'Your coffee's a long time coming.' she said. 'Must be gone to Brazil to pick the beans.'

Nodding to herself, she then told me about the dentist sitting two tables away. Said he was a real tooth fairy. The man over there by the window in the grey suit is a bank manager with a smelly bollocks.

'Don't ask me how I know.'

She turned her head, shifted position to look behind her, then swivelled back into place.

'Herself, that blond hoor there sitting beside the black lad, will let you ride her for a bag of chips and a burger. A cheese burger'd see her give you fair mileage.'

My coffee arrived. The waiter Charlie left without saying a word.

'Look at that cunt at the till giving us dirty stares.'

'How long are you here, Breege?'

'Since ten.'

'This morning?'

'Since the fuckers opened up.'

'You …' I think of the lie she said – about being in court this morning – but maybe she's confused? Yesterday morning? Or in court at nine and out ten minutes later?

'I can't stand to stay in the bedsit. Once I'm awake I'm out of it. Soon as. It does in my head if I've to look at the shitty walls for too long.'

'And – this is what you do all day. Buy food and not eat it?'

'I'll eat some and then head off – I'd be gone an

hour ago if that crabby hoor hadn't been shooting me dagger looks – to a pub, and sure I might get in with someone nice. Who knows. It's happened to me before, but I'm not able much for the mickey anymore, so it's blow-jobs and hand-shandies.'

'Breege – where are you going to end up?'

'It's all arranged – there's a bed waiting for me in the hospice. I worked there for a few years and sure the staff know me.'

'All thought out.'

She sighed. Said she'd planned her wedding to perfection but the day turned out to be a total fucking disaster. Rows and bloody rows – spent her honeymoon in a mobile home in Curracloe and had her first offside ride on the dunes with a Carlow man in a cowboy hat three days into her marriage. But sure what else could she do? She and drippy Dermot were skint and there wasn't a screed of food in the presses. Stay here, she told him. I'll get us money. And she did.

She always did.

She brought the fork to her mouth and began to eat. I downed the dregs of my coffee and said I had to go. She nodded, said I had to say a prayer for her, if I was into saying prayers. And then, curiously, she thanked me.

'I did nothing, Breege.'

'You're a sound man – I was in need of help a few years ago and you got it sorted. Made me a cup of tea and if your eyes were up my mini, at least your hands weren't, and you weren't sniggering at my shoes. There's not many who've treated me like I was their equal. I'm telling you. I have to fight and say I am. Equal. Everyone's got flaws but some fuckers go on as though they've got scented shite. Like her, that one …'

'Breege, that's life. Some are more equal than others – people look down their noses at other people. It happens to her behind the till, too.'

'No. She's cut me to the quick a couple of times I've come in here. Ignored my good mornings to her, my hellos. No fucking way. She did it a couple of days ago when I had Jamesy with me. I'll give her fucking reason to ignore me.'

Veering left outside the door, I turned and saw her through the P of Patsy's in the window glass. She was busy wagging her forefinger at your one with the up-turned nose. And if the movement of her lips was anything to go by, the air was bluer than a clear sky.

In her mind she was making herself heard. Equal. Except she's not, can never be. People like her don't start life on the bottom rung of a ladder – they start even lower and stay there.

But when I come to write her story I'll try not to end it like that. I'll make it so that she won some of her battles, made a difference, was equal. Or maybe I'll just have her house not fully painted and leave it at that.

Slow

I hear from Annette this evening. She calls just as I get in from work. Joe's upstairs, trying to rest before he goes on night duty. Annette's getting married, she says, to a Zulu. She's living in Durban, South Africa. I haven't seen her for eight years. I hope her new fella knows how to duck. Joe doesn't. His slow reactions cost him half an ear. Whenever he starts on at me I just tug on my ear lobe and he shuts up. He and Annette were an item long before I'd come on the scene. I was partly the reason for him being injured. But the main reason is Joe's slowness.

After the call I've to make myself a cup of tea. Usually I'd bring Joe up a cup. He likes his black with one sugar. Joe works with a security firm which usually employs oldish guys who can't get any other type of work. He works nights. Eight till eight, four nights a weeks; sometimes he does an extra shift. He gets paid under the counter for this. No tax. Sipping at my tea, I go over what Annette had said.

She wants me to visit her in South Africa in June. I suppose it's only natural for a sister to see another get married. Annette didn't attend my big day – I don't think it would have looked right, not the way things ended between her and Joe. She was lucky not to have done gaol.

I'd like to go see her get married. She's fifty-two and the man she's marrying is fifty-seven. Pastor Martin's his name. He's black, she said, with steel wool for hair and owns all of his teeth. Pearly white teeth the sun washes when he smiles. Annette said she sent on some photographs. Then she giggled like a schoolgirl and said not to mind how she looked in them. I asked her how she looked and she went four fathoms silent.

Fat, she said, not a thread of my red hair left. Missing a breast. I didn't know. I was quite shocked. But we'd fallen out for years, not speaking with each other. I think a bit of her will always love Joe. I said that to Joe once. He was drunk at the time. He said she'd got the bit of him she loved. His ear.

Her breast. She told me all about it. While she was talking I was feeling my own. Frightens me, it does, the thoughts of the Big C. I said I'd sooner die not knowing how it was happening. Thank you very much. She said I was hilarious. I asked her what her hair colour was. She said blonde. Bleached blonde. I have a picture of Annette in my mind. It's not very flattering. I hope she'll look better in her photographs.

I should call Joe. He needs to shave and shower before he climbs into his navy uniform. He annoys me when I see him polishing his peaker. The way he went on you'd think he'd an important job. I've lost track of the times I've told him he's only a security guard, a pushover skittle for the criminals. I mean, what could he do to stop a place being robbed? Nothing. He's too old, too thin, half-blind, half-deaf. All he does is check in, lock the door and read the paper, eat his lunch. He sleeps a lot. He's told me it's his depression. Joe says he's got a ringing noise in his ears, tinnitus. He used to serve as a gunner in the army. He says the big guns messed up his ears.

I didn't like him being in the army. He went out foreign too often. We needed the extra money but I think he'd have gone for nothing. At his unit dinner dance I heard someone asking him how the woodpecker was keeping. So I suspect he might have strayed once or twice. It used to bother me.

Most people suffering from tinnitus experience difficulty sleeping at night, so I doubt if Joe has it, but then he works most nights, so it's hard to say with him. He should be getting up. Then again he always looks tired the afternoons he is up, rings under his eyes. This morning he didn't eat the toast I'd popped for him, made a face at the tea I'd poured, asking if I'd poisoned it. I'm tired of telling him he's not able for these nights. You're not a young man anymore, I told him, but did he listen? He did not. Never listens. I'll let him rest for another while.

I love him, though. Always have. Expect I always will. He hasn't been an easy man to live with. If you annoy him he'll scrape the face off you with a scowl. He used to shout at the children but stopped when they started shouting back. Even now, they shout him down. He said they have no respect for him. He's right, but then he's only himself to blame, I told him. He knows exactly what I'm talking about, he does.

The woman he left me for, oh, about ten years ago, is dead. All my curses must have caught up with her on the same day. A large woman with bulgy sort of eyes and breasts that were too large to be decent. She was built like a roll-on, roll-off ferry. She dropped dead in the supermarket last month, in Dunnes Stores, with a cucumber in her hand. It'd be funny if it weren't true. I lit a candle for her in church, but it went out, so I relit it for someone else. Annette said I wasn't to harbour ill feelings towards the woman. That God knows we all make mistakes. Still, when I heard she'd died I hoped she'd dirty knickers on. She caused me a great deal of pain in her day. Joe never mentions her. He works with a brother of hers. He looks a lot like his sister, though his breasts aren't as big. I believe they don't get along, which must make Joe feel as if he's being haunted. Good enough for him.

I took up with Joe about a year after he broke up with Annette. We bumped into each other at a dance. He'd developed a habit of shielding his ear with his hand. He used to keep his hair mid-length to hide the injury, but he hasn't the hair to do that anymore. So he wears his ear now like a flag. Thinks it makes him look tough. That he'd tumbled with Mike Tyson instead of Mum's vase. A missile launched at speed by Annette. She'd got on to him about flirting with me, squeezing me in places. He'd tried to laugh it off and then he scowled at her. She took aim. Mum's flowers and the water, the floral-patterned vase, all spilt, shattered and splashed.

In company he says a mugger bit him. A black mugger – says the fucken country is getting like the Bronx.

He should have ducked, I told him, but he said he never saw it coming. I said that was half his problem: he never saw anything coming.

Annette has a daughter. I didn't know. She's called Milly, after me. I thought that was nice of Annette. That Pastor Martin must be good for her. She's let go of the past, never mentioned her money I spent. Money left to her by Mum. I simply didn't know where it got to. I just ate into it bit by bit. Ten thousand euro on a kitchen extension I didn't need, and then I spent Annette's share on a month's holiday in France. I love France. The Eiffel Tower and all.

The situation worsened because I burst the overdraft limit and Joe freaked. It took almost two years to get the account back into the black. I'm useless when it comes to dealing with money. And it's partly Joe's fault, too. If he hadn't been messing around with your one, he'd have kept an eye on the money. As it was he didn't care, once I said nothing about his carry-on. He took her away for weekends. I expect he did it on Annette's money. He could be spiteful like that – getting his own back on the pair of us. Annette for his ear, and me for just being his wife.

Speaking with Annette was a tonic. Like we were young again, at a time when we got along really well. But even then I remember she had a habit of throwing things. I sometimes wonder what would have happened if she hadn't thrown the vase. I think they'd have got married. But I don't think they'd have been happy. I think Joe would have felt like a plastic duck in a fairground, always being aimed at.

I really should be calling him. He might be collecting *her* brother, and need to leave a little earlier. They work in some factory outside Dublin.

Up the stairs. Creak the top one. Hit the landing light. That bathroom door – he'll never get round to painting it. Lazy so-and-so. Look at his sweater lying over the banisters, the inside-out shirt has a grimy neck. I spend my life telling him to leave his dirty washing in the linen basket under the stairs. Wasting my time I am. He never listens. He says he's going deaf. Points to his half-ear – as though to suggest if I've a problem I should take it up with Annette.

She ruptured his hearing. In fact, he says, she's the reason he can't claim for hearing-loss compensation against the Defence Department. I bet he didn't change his underwear before getting into bed. I bet he didn't even shower. I'll change the sheets when he's gone. I suspect that he's picking his nose in bed, too. If I ever catch him, it won't be a vase I'll hit him with.

'Joe ...'

No answer. Usually the bedside lamp would be on, and he'd be sitting up reading the paper, looking over the rim of his glasses at me, wondering what had kept me with the tea. The room's dark.

'Joe!'

After thumbing the switch my hand goes straight to my mouth. Joe's looking right at me through glassy eyes. The wisp of hair that was always falling in front of his face hangs as far as his nose. An ugly strip of grey hair. Joe. Joe with the missing ear, Joe shouting at his children shouting back at him. Joe with the floozy. Tender Joe, funny Joe. Deaf Joe. My Joe. Dead Joe.

I call the doctor, call the priest and will call a neighbour after I've breathed some prayers for my poor dead Joe. Knowing him, how slow he is, he probably doesn't yet know he won't be coming to South Africa with me.

The Mango War

We drive forklifts with long blades that lift hand-high and don't reach. They have computer screens telling us what to pick, the aisle number we have to drop the load at, the destination. Every destination carries a code number. Next week I'm travelling to see my mother in Roscommon or 4-5-6. I might well eat bananas I'd dropped in 4-5-6's aisle. In this sort of job you get to know what people like eating. Wexford people love Golden Delicious apples; Killarney people like pears; Galway people are partial to white seedless grapes. Everyone loves cherry tomatoes.

So we load wooden pallets with choice fruit and veg. We're allowed to stack eight boxes high. If you don't stack properly the boxes might tumble. If you turn a corner too fast the boxes will tumble. If you brake suddenly the boxes will tumble. Tumbles spoil goods and cause delays. And these are not good.

This wet Saturday I enter the warehouse and check the notice board. I find some of the new names on the work roster interesting: Colin Xing, Lawrence Dong,

Maximus Sold, Bright Sumahore. Whatever notices there are have been translated into Chinese. The main notice concerns a company night out at the local greyhound track, where wine and finger food will be available. I scribble my name and work number under Oliver Freeborn's.

Most of the people working in Fruit & Veg are foreigners: Chinese, Nigerians, Poles, Brazilians. You don't get to hear much English spoken in Fruit & Veg – sometimes a Pole will throw out a *Conas atá tu*? I can't remember an Irish person ever posing a question in Irish to me, outside of school that is.

The Chinese are the hardest workers. There are two old guys here. One is an Irish ex-soldier in his mid-forties. Strong but flabby. He works hard. He says he wants to lose weight, but he is damned if he's going to pay money to work out in a gym. Yorkie, he's called. After the chocolate bar. He's losing weight.

The other old guy is Fernando. He doesn't take breaks. He sneaks biscuits into his mouth from his coat pocket in the chill room. Fernando loses his cool if other forklifts prevent his from getting close to the stock. He likes to have his pallets right next to whatever he's picking. I've seen him and a Nigerian called Teddy almost come to blows in front of the mixed peppers. Teddy had refused to move his forklift out of Fernando's way.

At seven in the evening Fernando always asks the supervisor of the day if he can go home. I think it's because he's run out of biscuits. He eats chocolate chip cookies – I see the wrappers lying in the chill room aisles, between the iceberg lettuce and broccoli.

After we've loaded our pallets, we wrap plastic around the boxes so they don't fall when the drivers wheel them into their trucks. We write in permanent marker on the plastic our work number, destination code and aisle number. Blame has to lead back to someone. Once I forgot to load spring onions and courgettes and the customers of 5-3-4 kicked up a fuss. And the drivers can be bitchy if the loads aren't properly stacked or wrapped.

In the forklift bay I pick a machine, insert a universal key, check the battery strength and drive to the supervisor's station and pass my card across the clock-in machine. I type in my number on the forklift's screen and get my first pick of the day: 434 items heading for 2-3-4, Ballina, aisle 23.

I'm putting pallets on the blades when Fernando calls me. His craggy face is lined with bad news. The steel has worn through the leather skin in the toes of his work boots, which is an odd place for it to happen when you consider he's always kicking his heels.

'We must pick three hundred boxes an hour,' he says robotically.

'Three hundred boxes.'

'Yeah? Really?' I say.

He nods, 'Yeah, the supervisor say so. He say the Chinese pick five hundred boxes each hour. The Chinese, no good. No good.'

I don't come from a fruit and veg home. It was Fernando who introduced me to aubergines, avocados, papayas, courgettes, mangos. And explained the difference between honeydew melon and cantaloupe melon and put me on track when the screen's abbreviations confused me, in particular where tomatoes were concerned: beef, vine, with stem, without stem, cherry.

I feel sorry for Fernando. He's wiry but pushing on in years. He suffers when he has to lift boxes above his head – apples kill him, the Golden Delicious in particular as they're heavy and awkward.

Fernando glances at his watch, pinches his nose, then says, so I won't waste time looking for them, 'No apricots.' He steps aboard his forklift, heading for where the bananas are stored. Banana boxes are the foundations on which we build our loads.

I've promised myself to visit some of the places where the fruit and veg produce comes from: bananas from Surinam, pineapples from Ghana, kiwi fruit from Chile, Braeburn apples from New Zealand and so on. I always imagine that the fruit I handle was touched by a young woman and there is a connection there with us. You think about lots of things in order to break the monotony of this picking life.

We start our picks.

The supervisor rarely bothers us, only abandoning his station to check the aisles, and that pallets have been stacked properly, and that the Fruit & Veg area is tidy when the picks have been completed. Sometimes if we're short-staffed he'll pick a load, but he's very slow and falls far below the target he expects us to achieve.

At first break I feed the canteen vending machine with thirty cents and press D3 for a polystyrene cup of white and sugary coffee. Yorkie joins me at the table. He rubs his eyes and sips at his tea. The microwave pops and a blond-haired Chinese gets up for his chicken soup. All the Chinese sit at the one table, not saying much, but making lots of noise when eating.

Yorkie talks army. I'm trying to read my paper, an article about Roy Keane's return to the Irish soccer team. But Yorkie's voice is too strong to ignore. He has a son about my age. He likes to talk about him.

'He binge drinks, you know, smokes – doesn't go to Mass. Won't get up off his arse and find a job – it's not as if they're hard to find these days. Jesus, years ago they were like gold dust. He was in the army – lasted a week, no more. A week isn't long enough to decide whether or not you like something. Is it?'

Yorkie always has a lot to say. Finished talking, he looks at me, affording me the opportunity to speak. I doubt if he affords his son the same opportunity, or if he does, I think he closes his ears as to what his son has to say. I remain silent.

He asks if I'm going to the dogs on Friday night and I say I am. He says he might too. But I know he won't. Yorkie is forever saying he's going here or there, but in the end he doesn't go anywhere. I think the army's ruined him – he won't go anywhere unless he's marched there in a platoon.

I leave him to wallow in his disgruntlement and go outside to the Perspex fag point the firm attached to the warehouse to accommodate smokers. The likes of Yorkie and my father make me enjoy a puff all the more. They know how to spoil the living.

Back on the floor the blond Chinaman's load tumbles over after a mushroom box in the middle of his stack caves in under the weight of the watermelons. Anyone who is close by gives him a hand to gather up the spillage. Except Fernando, who drives on, shaking his head, disappointed at seeing us help someone whom he deems no good. We don't like those who pass fallers because we all fall and we feel embarrassed about it and having someone help you and you helping someone – well, it's the picker's unwritten rule, and liking or disliking a person doesn't come into it. But I guess people like Fernando can't let go of how they feel. And we all suffer because of it.

Later, Fernando's wrapping pallets with plastic. Teddy's stacking bags of red onions on a pallet of 7.5 kg potatoes. The Chinese have parked their forklifts in front of the rows of cucumbers and lemons and are huddled in a group, talking and gesticulating. Teddy walks over to me and says, 'Something's up. Something happened.'

His eyes draw mine to Fernando driving in the direction of the chill room.

'What happened?' I ask.

'One of the Chinese was hit on the back of his head.
A mango. He fired a mango.'

'Who?'

'Fernando.'

'Did they see him?'

Teddy shrugs, 'Maybe.'

I look over at the Chinese he'd hit. He's standing in
a group of his fellow countrymen. Very few speak
English while others have only a smattering. Mostly they
talk to us through smiles and nods and little else.

The guy has blood on his hand, is staring at it like he
can't believe it's his. One of the Chinese arrives on a
forklift and hands a medical kit to the oldest Chinese,
and he applies a wipe and then a pack to the guy's
wound. The others yap like crazy and then drive into
the chill room where the iceberg lettuce and mush-
rooms are kept.

Teddy says, 'Shouldn't we do something?'

Yorkie says, 'No. We'll come back in a few minutes
and do what we have to.'

I think that already it's too late to help Fernando.
And it is. I hear the forklifts emerging from the chill
room. Fernando is lying naked on two pallets on his
own forklift, his mouth taped, his wrists and ankles
spread-eagled and bound by wrapping. His eyes scream
for help. The Chinese driver looks straight ahead and
carries on towards the freezer. Minutes later he returns
on another forklift. They resume work as though
nothing had happened. The injured party is all smiles.

Fernando could freeze to death in there.

Yorkie's in the freezer, pulling the masking tape from Fernando's mouth. Teddy's cutting the wrapping off — some of the workers in the freezer, geared up in blue quilted suits and gloves, stand around laughing. We help Fernando to his feet. His skin is pale and his teeth chatter. He hides his eyes from us. Teddy hands him a black sack to cover his bits. Yorkie drives Fernando to his clothes in the chill room. He dresses quickly, shaking all over. Perhaps from the fright more so than the cold.

When he's dressed he drives to the supervisor's station and swipes his card across the machine.

Yorkie says, 'I bet he'll quit.'

We all hope he does.

Teddy says, 'Yeah, you don't mess with the Chinese.'

Yorkie nods, 'And what happens next, if he doesn't?'

Teddy says, 'Next?'

'Yeah, if they fall out with each other and one pops the other with a mango and blames you, me or Barry here?'

Not so ridiculous a notion, I decide, after first thinking he'd watched *The Godfather* movies too often.

That's how the alliance came about: a coalition of Irish, Brazilian, Nigerian and Polish, for Fernando didn't quit. Reluctantly, we're on his side.

The supervisor has caught the tension in the air. Often he appears in Fruit & Veg on a new forklift, eyes searching for anything unusual. Meanwhile, Fernando eats his cookies and waits, a mango in his jacket pocket.

Dream Horse

The air smells of furze, of approaching spring, of a prolonged winter. In the distance the Wicklow hills are snow-encrusted; behind them the sky a canvas of blue. I suppose it's too soon to be here. Sorting out Dad's things, sorting out the debris of his life. He's a week dead. The cottage isn't his. It came with the job for as long as the job was his. The new man is waiting to put his feet under the table.

Racehorses clip-clop past the window as they do every morning, no matter what the weather, no matter what day it is. The lads aboard them chat about this and that. I don't know how they stick the cold, or tolerate the rain that comes at them in driving sheets as they thunder up the gallops. But today it isn't raining. Today it's just cold. Today isn't so bad.

The cottage, the job, gave Dad the opportunity to move away from us, to leave Mum. They didn't get on for a long time. They argued and fought like a cat and a dog with tails tied together. If our walls could talk, they'd shout.

Mum suspected him of having a fling with a woman half his age. True or not, I don't know. Or care. He wasn't cruel or overly kind. His sins are buried with him. A small man, round-faced, with eyes that always had a sheen of unspecified sorrow in them. Regret, disappointment, guilt? I don't know. Perhaps a drop of each in his pale blue eyes.

The cottage is tidy, which is unusual for him. He was not a tidy man. The newspaper he was reading when he had the heart attack is folded on the coffee table in the sitting room. There's a photograph of him on the mantelpiece, smiling face pressed against that of a horse's. The way it is you'd think the grey-headed horse is smiling too. Perhaps Dad had told him he was stud-bound.

I boil up his kettle for coffee. Most of his things are packed and in the trailer out front, ready for the county-council dump. The things I want to keep I've placed in the car. His car. A battered old Toyota with a wheeze in its engine and a dirty tongue of an exhaust.

The kettle's red button pops. I add a modicum of milk, and a spoon of instant coffee to a mug and stir. I sip slowly, the chipped part of the mug rough against my lip. Out back there are winter flowers in hanging baskets. I'll leave them. Dad wasn't into flowers.

The bathroom's clean. Spotless. Jasmine scent and blue loo, a roll of pink toilet paper with finger indentations. The walls are covered with a jaded floral paper. There are patches of mildew in places. The cottage has those round pin plugs and sockets. There's a nail from which a painting of Dad and his favourite horse used to hang. Gone now. If I had a choice of something to remember him by, I'd have chosen that.

A holy-water stoup with a dried-up sponge is next to the front door. Dad wasn't a man to dip his fingers in water. Gin was a different proposition.

Visiting the cottage after he'd moved in, I was struck at how relaxed in himself he'd become – like a soldier home from a dangerous front. I knew by his mien, the way in which his shoulders no longer climbed, that as Mum's peace envoy I was wasting my time. So I didn't ask him to come home. I couldn't look him in the eye and put the request to him. Not because I didn't want him home, but because I sensed that it was not right for him. Sometimes the scars of a bad marriage know no healing.

The work at the stud kept him active, not too busy, he said. Still, I could tell by him that he missed the buzz of the training stable, missed the chatter of the lads, missed trying to suss out a horse's character. As a child I thought there was something magical, something lyrical and timeless and soul-inspiring about horses – that without them heaven would not be heaven. But, keen as I was to follow in Dad's footsteps, he shepherded me from his calling.

During a trip to his yard, his boss asked me what weight I was. Dad cut in, saying I was too heavy and had Grandad's long legs. I resented his lack of enthusiasm and sulked all the way home, raised nothing more than a mutter to his Band-Aid apologetics and explanations about how dangerous, how hard a life his profession could be. From there on in he made a point of exhibiting his wounds: the deep bites from a horse on his arm, the kick beneath the eye. Mentioned too, a young fella who'd died from a fall from a horse.

He smoked Hamlet cigars. The mild sort that might give you a mild form of cancer, Mum said. Dad liked his gin without tonic, his brandy neat, too. He wore suits on Curragh racing days. He brought home strange friends. A German doctor and his wife who smoked cigarettes that left a thick smell in the air. A man called Black George who inked over the Pope's eyes in a newspaper photograph. A Canadian jockey whose nerves were sellotaped together with cigarettes and booze.

Dad once told me, when he was a little steamed – we only had conversations when he was tipsy – that I was a good lad. A fine son. He asked me what I was going to do with my life. I shook my head. You don't know at thirteen.

'Leave,' he said, 'go to America. There's nothing here, only hard work and low pay. And it'll not get better, mark my words. I can fix things for you – you think I'm drunk, don't you? Well, I'm not. When you're old enough and you want to go, tell me. Listen to your mam and you'll end up pumping petrol into other men's cars – fellas that wouldn't be half the human you are.'

On other days, when his blood was alcohol free, I'd have needed a claw hammer to prise words from him.

He almost made the grade as a top-flight jockey. His dream horse came along. A classy chestnut gelding that had pulverised the opposition in its first four races. A horse that died during an operation to correct a minor breathing difficulty. There were other horses, but Dad never forgot his dream horse.

Newspaper articles remark about the chemistry between Dad and his horse. Dad said that sometimes an animal can come to mean too much to a man. Other horses made him comfortably off. He was neither mean nor generous, but he never shirked a hand from his pocket when someone was stuck for a few bob.

He brought me to Tipperary racecourse where he was riding in a veterans' race. He could scarcely conceal his excitement. The years were rolled back, the wrinkles smoothed over. I'd wondered why he'd been shedding weight, had eased up on the booze and visited saunas. I got the impression that he was pleased to be giving me a glimpse of his life, a part he held dearly. Keep one eye on the future and one on the past, he told me, that way you can live in the present. Mum said he was Solomon talking through his behind.

Funny. I thought it funny to see him in green diamond silks. I'd never seen him wearing silks before. In photographs, yes. But not in the flesh, not with my own eyes. He had a racing sweater at home, a beige cotton garment that the owner of his dream horse had given him. I have newspaper cuttings and a photograph of the pair clearing a Punchestown fence. They adorn a wall in my New York apartment. Because the horse was important to him, it's important to me.

He didn't win the vets' race. Finished third. He really enjoyed himself. He missed the buzz – had forgotten the broken bones, the wet, cold mornings, the occasions when horses under him were gambled on and failed to win. Time dusts over bad times, gilds with fool's gold the good old days. Another favourite from Solomon's behind.

He left home shortly afterwards. He'd had enough of Mum's contrary ways, her eagerness to argue, her prolonged stiff silences. He apologised to the lot of us, but that didn't stop the others from turning against him. Six months later he met Phil, so he never got to play the Prodigal Father. I'd often harboured the notion that Dad and Mum might remember the road they'd travelled together, but it was a childish wish.

Black George was at the funeral, thinner than I remembered, wrinkled-up eyes matching his wrinkled-up clothes. The Canadian jockey came too, with a new wife on his arm, his hair slicked and polished. He said Dad was there for him when his saddle was soapy. Black George said nothing, yet said it all with a grimace. Watching them go was sad, links with childhood disappearing, carrying with them stories of the man amongst his own friends. I envied them for knowing my father in a way I never could.

My meeting with Phil for the first time caused Dad considerable embarrassment. She came in through the door as I was about to leave, her own key in her hand. She smiled and asked me to stay for dinner, as if my staying meant everything to her. And I did, even though it was getting late, and I knew the inquisition from Mum was waiting to start the moment I got home. She loved horses, she said. And Dad; ach, you could see it in her eyes.

Phil wore black at the funeral and held a single red rose. She carried herself with a quiet dignity. And I thought of Mum sitting at home with her memories, tears keeping her company but not softening her heart. I didn't know for which of the two I felt sorriest.

Later, at the cottage, Phil brewed tea and stared through the window at the pipework of trees at the bottom of the garden. We said little at first, but then she softened and told me things, things that struck a chord with me. Funny things he didn't know were funny – things I sometimes fought to bury a smile at so as not to hurt his feelings. And his eyebrows, God, he spoke with them the way some people do with their hands. Up and down they'd go, especially when he was awaiting a response to some of his Solomon's wisdom.

Phil's upstairs now in the bedroom, taking her mind for a walk through happier days. Dad and Phil were strangers to the people in each other's past lives.

It was Phil who rang me with the news of Dad's sudden death. I was his only son, the only member of his family to attend the funeral services; still, you'll have that in small places with no forgiveness. Mum said that Dad was dead a long time for her.

Phil's a pleasant sort; short dark hair, hazel eyes, leaning towards heaviness. I don't know how he's left her fixed. I hope she's somewhere to go, a few euros in the bank. I'd ask but it'd feel like an intrusion.

She closes the bedroom door behind her. Her foot creaks the bottom stair. I think of the clean bathroom, the effort she put into leaving a respectable place for a stranger. Her eyes are red-rimmed, cheeks puffy. She nods. It's time.

She carries a brown suitcase and a painting wrapped in cardboard sheeting and tied with blue string. Her eyes are possessive, but I've no intention of asking her about it. I ask instead if there's somewhere I can drop her: a bus stop, train station. She shakes her head.

'No,' she says, 'I'll be fine, thanks anyhow.'

I think she wants to remember with whom she was last in the car. It's a pity she can't drive, a pity the engine's on its uppers.

I slam the front door and drop the key in the letterbox. Dad's car starts noisily, belches black smoke. I pass Phil at the bus stop. She gives a tight final wave goodbye.

I take the Tipperary road. The racecourse where I park is empty and bleak. If I listen carefully, strain my ears above the din of a Sprite can being chased by the wind, I can hear the thunder of hooves.

The Thing Is

An unusual family. Us. There's Dad who doesn't talk, and Mum who does. There's Gina who's sad, and Karen who's not. There's Victor who's intelligent, and me who isn't. There was also Adam, who's not anything anymore, and this is what this is all about.

We live in a large bungalow set in a corner of a field, near a crossroads. Dad farmed sheep and also trained two racehorses. He did neither very well. We survived on what he made from selling off bits of the land.

Mum tends to her face a lot. Fighting wrinkle advancement on every front with all sorts of creams. She's losing the battle around her eyes, where the lines are deep. Dad used to tell her she could no sooner push back time than he could his belly button. Mum doesn't speak with him all that much. They act like people who are extremely fed up with each other, and don't know what to do about it. Dad is very small in Mum's eyes and has been for a long time. We didn't think he could get any smaller. But he did.

In the week leading up to what happened to Adam, Gina told us all she was pregnant. She's a very attractive redhead with a smooth figure. She wasn't happy with her breasts though; I'd caught her a couple of times feeling herself in the mirror, and sighing this way and that, as if she were half-afraid of discovering something. An aunt of ours died before Christmas and it affected all the women in our house something dreadful. Mum stockpiled all into the jeep and drove into Doc Harrison in Kildare, who got them appointments in a Dublin hospital. That's next week. The appointments were put back on account of what happened to Adam.

Mum's about the worst affected. It was her sister who had died. And they looked alike. She told Dad it was like looking at herself lying in the coffin. Of course, Dad had no drink in him, so he said nothing, just sat there in his armchair by the range, smoking his pipe. Probably wishing to himself that it was Mum.

He said nothing when Gina said she was pregnant. His hooded eyes appeared to dim and his cheeks went hard. You'd think someone had tightened a screw on his lips they got so tight. We thought he would lose his temper. Sometime he does. Over nothing. He'd be so quiet in himself, and then get completely thick about something: the TV too loud, or someone leaving a smell in the loo, stuff like that.

Pregnant. Jesus.

Mum's hands shot to her temples. Karen buried a nervous smile. Victor looked up from his book. Victor was reading *Robinson Crusoe*. Must be for the fortieth time. He loved the idea of being away on a desert island, away from everyone. Though he said he'd have a preference for a Woman Friday. He said the author might have been a little queer to think up a Man Friday in the first place. Though, the times he lived in might have had some bearing on his decision. They liked to keep the lid on their shit back then.

We're twins. I'm thirteen years, four months and three days old. He's two minutes older. He says on the way out he grabbed the only brains on offer. Karen says he grabbed the good looks, too. She said that to spite me. But Victor is handsome. He has jet black hair, lean features and large blue eyes you'd think a clear sky had spat into.

My hair isn't so dark, my features not so lean. My nose – well, Victor says whoever had it last time must have been a boxer. A bad one.

Adam had his own room. He used to hand his shoes down to Dad. Mum blames the chemicals in the food chain for the kids being so tall these days; big-feeted kids, she says, when she's full of Bailey's. Talking about Adam's yacht-sized footwear parked under the stairs.

'Pregnant!' Mum shrieked.

Gina bit her lower lip. Nodded

'Who?' Mum said.

'Terry.'

She said Terry as if the lot of us should know him. Adam looked at me, moved his fair eyebrows up and down. He was sixteen and a half. He'd fiery pimples and loved watching the wrestling on TV. He'd light fairish hair which he kept smoothing and it was always gelled. Sometimes he put dyes in his fringe: blue and pink. His favourite wrestler was The Undertaker. Dad hates the sport. Says it's played by Nancy boys, and the whole thing is just a rig-up. We think he's so anti-wrestling because it was Adam's hobby. And Adam thought so, too.

Dad jumped to his feet, his eyes full of storms. It's as though he's disgusted with the lot of us for Gina getting herself pregnant. He left the kitchen.

'Terry who?' Mum said, trying to keep calm. The fat of her upper arms jiggled and I think how the needle mark on her arm looked like a third eye.

Gina thumbed her hair behind her ears. She has big ears, which is a good reason for wearing long hair. Karen's ears aren't so big, so her hair is tight. She likes to wear earrings and sometimes a stud in her nose.

'Magee,' Gina breathed.

You'd know Gina was lying. But you'd have to know her to know. A signpost doesn't come up on her head to tell you. Her soul has little ingredients: a drop of blush on her cheeks, a line of worry down her forehead, the way her forefinger touches the corner of her lip. Mum knows how to read the signs, too. But she lets on she doesn't. I think it's because she can read other signs I haven't learned to read yet.

Then Adam slunk away, shoulders hunched. He used to suffer from asthma, and kept an inhaler in his pocket.

We used count on him going into hospital for a week every year, mostly when the fog rolled down from the mountain, or in summer when the sun was blistering. But he sort of grew out of it during a time when everyone thought he'd have asthma forever. The way Dad used to look at him was like a sun worshipper taking in a dull day. Victor says it's because Adam was almost a man and would have looked at Dad through a man's eyes, and Dad knew he wouldn't pass for being a man in his eldest son's eyes.

Karen shook her head. She's not really into fellas, she says. She's never going to get married or have babies. Ever. She used to like playing with my action men. Victor said it was because Action Man had no penis, and therefore did not constitute a threat to her.

Mum said to Karen, 'Do you know him?'

Karen shook her head. She sat on her knees on the chair, elbows on the table, hands supporting her chin, looking at Gina in a curious sort of way. Taking in her lie. She can read Gina, too.

'Where did you meet him?' Mum said, setting out to take apart Gina's lie.

'At a disco … Nijinski's.'

'When?'

'We've been going with each other for about a month.'

'Do you know where he lives?'

Gina froze. Broke down. Tears streaming down her cheeks. Her shuddering something terrible. Her hands slapping her face, and when that didn't hurt her enough, they started tugging at her lovely red hair. Mum and Karen pulled at her, trying to get her to stop, which I thought was all weird, given that Gina was doing to herself what Mum wanted to do to her. They stopped her just as Victor touched my arm and nodded for us to leave.

That's something I like about Victor. He knows when it's the right time to leave. He doesn't wait to be told, like I normally do. In our bedroom, he climbed on to the top bunk. The springs squeaked like crazy. The bunks were bought from a neighbour's Going Away to a Madhouse Clearance Sale.

Mrs Travis lived about a mile away in a sorry-looking cottage with the best orchard for miles around. Victor said she held these sales every time the world got her down, which was becoming a fairly frequent occurrence. She was found wandering the roads in her nightdress and her family had her committed. Everyone was worrying about her carrying the Finnish moose-skinning knife. It belonged to her husband who Mum said was half-Finnish and loved to saunaise. Nothing will convince Victor that the old lady wasn't on her way to kill the two of us retired orchard robbers. We were responsible for her having a wall built around her apple farm, and when a storm blew some bricks onto her leg, breaking it, she never fully recovered. Sometimes when the wind blows hard and rain ticks against the window, I imagine the old lady's on the road, limping towards our house, brandishing that sharp, shiny knife. The rain falling silvery on her mad face. Coming to deball us, as Victor likes to say.

Victor sighed. And I couldn't see him do it but I was sure he was picking his nose. His voice sounded muffled. Sometimes it bugs me just to know people are doing something even though I can't see or hear them. I told him to quit.

'I only do it when I'm thinking hard.'

'Yeah, what are you thinking hard about now?'

I knew it wasn't Robinson Crusoe or Mrs Travis.

'There's no such person as Terry Magee.'

'How do you know that, Victor?'

'I just do. It doesn't take a genius.'

Then he said he was going asleep, which meant he wasn't but that he didn't want me disturbing him. When Victor doesn't want to talk, it means there's something really serious on his mind.

Sleep came in fits and starts. In the middle of the night I heard Karen shushing Gina to quieten her tears, telling her everything will be OK. Mum wasn't up. These nights she sleeps in the utility room. She'd told us that Dad's snoring drove her crazy. He didn't seem to mind her absence too much, and Mum didn't harp on about his visits to Dublin, where he stayed in a hotel to meet his old rugby friends. Victor said Adam told him that Dad hung his dirty linen on someone else's clothesline. Victor said he'd never seen Dad watch a rugby match on TV, or go to see one being played. He wouldn't even watch Ireland playing on the TV, not even if they were winning.

In the morning Adam wouldn't get out of bed when Dad called him. He kept the key turned in the lock and said nothing. Dad said three sheep were slaughtered by dogs in the fox covert and he needed Adam's help to cart them away. He wouldn't look for us, because Mum said that Saturday mornings were a study period for us, Easter Holidays and all other holidays included. Adam wasn't so bright in school. Mum used send him to Mrs Travis for grinds, and while he improved he still didn't get good enough grades. Mum said she wanted us to get into the habit of working hard.

Mum sat at the bay window, staring at the apple blossoms blowing across the yard like pink snowflakes. I wondered if she was mad at me for not picking up the lawn shavings. Victor had said to leave the grass. It had begun to rain. I don't mind the rain so much, but Victor said I should, because rain wore people down, made them old and bent over before their time. I think it was just an excuse to quit work early. Victor's a little lazy, I've noticed. But twins are twins, and we stick together, and I listen to him, because he wasn't born first for nothing.

Mum sipped at her tea. We didn't like her silence. She looked wicked. Pursed lips, uncombed hair, wrinkles rich and plenty like weeds in a garden left untended.

When Gina and Karen came in, Mum didn't stop looking through the window glass, and said, 'Who?'

Gina didn't answer. Mum made a go for her. Gina's not the smartest, but she was smart enough to keep the length of the kitchen table from Mum. I haven't seen Mum so mad since she found a hotel bill for two in Dad's pocket. She went looper then, and she moved into the utility room. Dad hit Mum once during those awful weeks of tension. Mum's brothers appeared on the doorstep one morning and collared Dad, leading him away somewhere. When he came back he was hardly able to walk. His lips were cut and his nose was a mess. Victor believes that Mum's brothers are in the IRA. I don't know if that's true, but I do know that sometimes we have strangers staying in the house, and Dad doesn't like it one bit.

'Who?' Mum screamed.

Victor nudged me, but I couldn't bring myself to move.

'Who?' Mum said, a step off a scream, hands shovelling her brown hair.

Karen glanced at Gina and said, 'I know.'

Silence, as Mum glared at Karen, her eyes like a vice grip. It seemed to me that Mum knew who the father was, but just needed to hear the name said out loud.

'I won't ask again,' Mam said, which she didn't mean because she was never going to stop asking. Karen let the name out with a cry and half-screech. Victor paled. My insides felt sick.

'No, no … no,' Mum said, as if every bit of wind behind her sails had died.

Dad!

Victor and me – well, we were sickened. The three women started to cry, and hug each other and all that. Victor and me, we felt as though we were somehow guilty of something. Later, Victor told me that men doing what Dad did gave decent mickies like us a hard time. That when women get mad with a bad man they lump us all together, and what Dad had done was something really awful.

Adam rushed in. He had been drinking. You could see it in his eyes, the red rings under them. He smoked hash, too, so Victor said. He supposed Adam had to do something in life to take his mind off following in Dad's sheepshit-stained wellies. There was a flicker of hope in his eyes, as though someone he hated had died and he'd come to outwardly grieve but inwardly smile.

'What's going on?' he said, cautiously.

He only wore boxer shorts. No one answered him. No one wanted to tell him.

'It's him, isn't it?' he said, his lips curling.

No one answered. No one said anything till he said he was going to get the fucking shotgun and blow him away. Then we all broke out laughing after Gina said there were no cartridges. She'd looked. Perhaps, if there were, then she'd have killed Dad, and if she had killed Dad, then maybe Adam would be alive today.

After the laughing finished, we all quietened. The

jeep filled some of our kitchen window, and Dad and the collie were climbing out, making their way round the gable end.

When he came in he took off his cap, touched the side of the teapot. Noticing the silence he sniffled and said, 'Bloody dogs worrying the shee—'

'You bastard!' Mum said, her eyes scalding.

'What?' Dad nodded, then pulled a face.

'These things happen … I'd a bit of drink on me, you …'

His eyes were all over the place. His tongue fell from his mouth, as though suddenly his mouth wasn't big enough to hold it. Mum lunged at him but he pushed her away, knocking her to the floor. A shocked look on her face at her own lightness. Victor watched none of this. He said he was studying Adam. How the vein in his neck throbbed, how grey with rage he'd become. After attacking Dad, Adam ended up holding his jaw, the girls rushing to stand between him and Dad.

We went to Mum and helped her to her feet. Dad left then, kicking at the door on his way out. We haven't seen him since. We know he emptied the bank account and flogged the jeep and the sheep. The racehorses, he left, which sums up their usefulness. We don't expect he'll be back. There's too many wanting to see him, too many wanting to put more than a word in his ear.

Adam went missing the next day. Victor said something had snapped inside him. He was found hanging from a tree in Mrs Travis's orchard. He left a letter for

Mum, told her things he didn't mind her knowing now that he was dead. Other things Dad had done.

Victor goes in to Adam's room a lot. Stays there for hours. I'm glad he's the twin with the brains, because I wouldn't like to see the things he sees. I'd like to tell him that just because he's intelligent doesn't mean he'll find all the answers. But I say nothing. Victor hasn't got enough respect for me to take my advice.

We miss Adam. The new baby no one can quite take to, yet. The thing is, it would have helped matters had he looked more like Gina.

Elliot's Really Dead

Elliot arrived home in a crate, on an El Al flight that was delayed by two hours in London because of some security hitch. Not that, if anything had gone wrong, Elliot would have cared. He was beyond caring about anything, except maybe missing the in-flight meal.

We walked into the huge hangar and went to the wooden crate with the Hebrew markings, a plywood box of the sort you'd expect to find oranges in, or bananas. George said Elliot's going to smell like shit fried in Bucharest, and another guy, Henry, who had a black spot on his lungs, and was waiting to be told all about it tomorrow, dished out surgical gloves, saying we should take precautions. He was right, I supposed, seeing as we didn't know what had killed Elliot.

Alfie, Elliot's soldier brother, broke the news to us last week as an aside. We were sitting in Neeson's Pub when he said, 'Elliot is dead.' Then he smiled. We all smiled. George shook his head and said Elliot never changed. George; we wonder about him, sometimes.

But our lips froze over and tongues seized up when it looked for real that Elliot was dead.

Elliot had already called work on three occasions to say he was dead. First time we all clubbed in and bought a huge wreath; second time the factory boss closed up early and sent us round to his mum's, a sweet old thing called Martha O'Leary, whose great-grandaddy left Ireland on a Famine ship and came home years later with Yankee gold he'd looted during his fighting days with the Confederate Army. A nice old woman who gave us tea and digestive biscuits and who laughed herself silly when told about poor Elliot. Second time round we learned Elliot used to make those calls himself. Third time he rang in no one did anything, and he ended up getting the sack. But the boss loved him and rehired him the following week. Elliot had charisma; not much else, but he had that.

We were close for a while. I think he felt he'd something in common with me being a Yankee and all. My wife's Irish, from County Roscommon, and that's why I'm over here. I like it, considering. I'm real proud of myself the way I've stayed married to the same woman for six years. It's a kind of a record in our family. My dad's side usually go through five marriages and five houses before they go sunny side down.

Henry sniffled and told George the Romanian to lever the lid. George is a little weasel of a guy, snivelly, the sort who'd wipe your ass if you asked.

'Go on … aren't you crowd used to doing that stuff

… didn't ya tell us all about Dracula, and how you know where he lived and all?'

I could see George was sweating on this one, so I said I'd pop the lid. No sweat. Why not? Odds were real that Elliot wasn't inside. So I took the jemmy from Henry and told the guys to stand back. The nails popped easily enough, and when I had them all out we looked at each other the way guys do when there's something shitty to be done and each is waiting for the other to make a move. But it was still my call so I grabbed the lid and put it to one side.

It was Elliot all right. No doubt. He was grey as cloud, and his chin was slack, and we could see the dark hole of his mouth. Henry said he could never keep his mouth shut, at which a bluebottle buzzed from Elliot's gob and sat on his fat upper lip. Henry stepped back. George blessed himself. These guys weren't used to seeing cadavers, but I'd seen enough in 'Nam so I didn't make much of a fuss. It's always harder when it's someone you know, but I just thought of his hand on my wife's ass, and it being Elliot there didn't bother me one bit.

So we looked him up and down for a few minutes. He wore a white angel dress and an ID tag around his big toe. He had dirt under his toenails, and one of the little ones was black where he must have let something fall on it. His mop of brown hair was a mess and a fringe fell like a string curtain over his closed eyes. He'd had large round eyes with a shake of brown and green in one iris, and the other a gooseberry green. They were closed now, shut tight – I just imagined the colours.

George said, 'He looks peaceful, yes?'

Henry said, 'He's really dead this time – certainly looks it.'

'Yeah, he's dead, a stiff dick,' I said. Then I told George to get on the mobile to the undertakers and remind them to bring the gear. We'd chipped in and bought Elliot a denim suit. We were going to dress him like the song says, 'Forever in blue jeans'. They were too long in the leg but as Henry said, no one looks at your feet when you're dead.

The undertakers' headlights lighted up a space between the hangar's double doors, and one of them got out and slid the doors fully apart. They drove through. The hearse gleamed and the coffin in the back was of a dark wood with small angels sitting on its lid. Kinda cute.

The taller of the pair came up to me and I told him the doc had already viewed the body and signed all he had to sign on the dotted line. I didn't know if he wanted to know that, but I hoped he did.

The shorter guy had the denim gear I'd given him earlier. I didn't think it'd be the done thing for us to have walked through the Airport Mortuary with the gear. You could have people conjuring up all sorts of things in their heads. Like is Elliot back there in the nude? Are they really going to dress him up in that? I know Ata had a pink tracksuit in mind but Elliot wouldn't have cared too much for it. He might have parked his feet on either side of the fence but clothes-wise he was as straight as they come. The tall guy put a scissors along the back of the jacket, cut along its middle, and then he did the same with the jeans. All the time he was talking away in a soft voice about Elliot, asking us what was he like, his line of work, what happened to him, looking at each of us without dropping a snip as we took turns to answer.

'You don't know what he died from?' he said, taking in his shorter companion, then focusing on our surgical gloves.

'No idea,' I said.

'The doctor …'

'He hasn't a clue … he's gone to get the Hebrew Death Cert translated.'

The tall man handed Henry the clothes. I think he would have dressed Elliot for us if he'd known what he died from – that it wasn't contagious.

I stuck the bit of collar we had cut off the shirt on Elliot's neck and then lifted him under the shoulders and raised him up a little, holding him while Henry and George slipped on a jacket sleeve each and joined the rip at the back; well almost, not that it mattered, as Elliot wasn't going to be showing his back to anyone anymore.

He smelt real bad, and a couple of times one of us had to break away and get some air. But eventually we got the job done and hoisted him into the coffin. Not being smart but he was a dead weight. Still, we were happy that we'd dickied him up as best we could, though sugar on shit doesn't sweeten the taste any. His hand on my wife's ass, and she leaving it there.

There was snow in his hair, and it took a lot of combing to get the stuff out, but we managed it OK. If Ata had been strong we could have let him in to do a proper job on his hair, but he woulda just freaked out.

The hearse backed out of the hangar and drove the short distance to the Airport Mortuary. We hurried and caught up with it and carried the coffin inside and put it down on a table in a room that was curtained off from the mourners. I removed the lid and went outside for a smoke, not going back indoors until after the prayers were done and everyone had seen enough of Elliot to convince themselves that this time he was really dead.

Then the doc came over, smiling, and told us it was OK, not to worry, that Elliot had only died from a heart attack.

'He was out jogging, not far from his apartment in Tel Aviv, when he had it. He was D.O.A. at the hospital.'

I'm sure Elliot was pleased to know he only died from a heart attack. In truth we were relieved, too. We all had families and jobs to keep. Last thing any of us needed was everyone freaking out because of some crazy goddamn Elliot epidemic.

Ata blubbered a lot. He was into letting it all hang out. After the prayers dived into a low drone and ended, there was that dreaded silence when it sank in that everyone needed to shift ass. A queue formed and people came up and blessed themselves over Elliot, saying something kind, before moving on through the door and falling in around the steps, at the end of which the wagon was quietly revving, fumes greying the night air.

So, Elliot's buried, and it's sad and all, but we get on with our lives, right? And no one sees what's coming when the boss arrives down on the factory floor about a month later and tells us he'd just got a call to say that Elliot's dead, that he died last night. Someone's idea of a joke, perhaps, but maybe not. Maybe it's someone just keeping his name alive, which sounds a weird way to do it, but then Elliot would appreciate that. He liked that sort of stuff.

Kafra

Harry Kyle dreams about thorns of Christ growing briary on the roadside, of air sweetened by orange and lemon groves, of banana plantations, fruit bagged in garish blue plastic, protection against heavy winter rains, yellow sandstorms, the sea's withering breezes and an added bitter coldness that falls with the darkening of day. Dreams of mushy terracotta soil, drying under the wild caress of a Mount Hermon wind. Of a pale sun in grey-white cloud, hundreds of seabirds raising a cacophony, feeding on the remains of a harvest reaped by gelignite fishermen.

His dream eye sees grey Israeli patrol vessels bobbing on a shoreline not theirs, passing the gaping eye socket of a Moorish keep, its sun-scorched walls soaking in the smoky aroma of mint leaves burned by loved ones of loved ones who can love no more, burned in a Muslim cemetery that reaches as far as tall iron gates set like black teeth between marble columns. The cry of the gannet, the shush to shore of stormy waves, the first time to see another's blood on his hand

and how it hurt, without causing him actual, physical pain.

Night has drawn in by the time he parks the Chevrolet jeep and unloads his pistol, returning the Browning to stores, along with Joe's Sten gun. He wakes then with a wide-eyed jolt and a constricting sensation in his throat. His sweat rich, thick and warm on his forehead, his temple veins throbbing. His dream ending as it had begun, with soap staining his hands a bright red.

Harry Kyle stares at the darkness until the darkness stares back. A stiff wind blows, sweeping across the Curragh Plains, blowing flecks of rain against the new PVC windows. June's naked buttocks lean in to his and he snatches comfort in her heat for a few moments before easing from bed.

In the kitchen he makes tea and brings the steaming mug into the living room and sits on a fireside chair, a breath of cold ash catching in his lungs. He sees the darkness and the amber streetlights of the Curragh Camp through the quarter of window revealed by the blind. The wind plays down the throat of the chimney, and sometimes it falls silent. Its silence is a silence of the ages, of wisdom garnered from the four corners of the world. In its silence Harry Kyle feels truly alone.

Since his return, June's trying to figure out what the hell has got into him. Why he has a mourning bell for a face, and why, sometimes, when disturbed by the kids, he yells at them and at her, and what happened to his relaxed, easygoing manner? He asks himself, too. Continually.

He is home from a place he couldn't wait to leave behind. And now, by night, and when not otherwise preoccupied, by day, he finds himself in his combat boots, reliving, and thinking, and when not thinking, seeing.

He's put on a little weight that June said suited him, has given her something to hold. He hadn't been training, he said. He is twenty-eight and used to like to pump iron, see the muscles flex in his forearms, feel the perspiration trickle down his spine. But the inclination to train had deserted.

He can never wash his hands enough. June appreciates that, the new ultra-hygienic Harry. You could eat your dinner off his hands if you didn't mind the smell of Dettol.

Home three weeks now but not home. His mind elsewhere, his grey eyes fastened on a Lebanese skyline, his nostrils taking in the rich red earth baked by the hot khamsin winds, freshened by the early autumn rains and a sea breeze that chased cracks in the hot winds, making crevices for the rains to come through.

Three Saturdays ago, he woke in his prefab accommodation and lay on for a few minutes. A brown army blanket tacked across the window blocked daylight, except for a tear in the middle that revealed a single bright eye. Reaching a hand from under the green mosquito netting, he thumbed a switch on his red Sharp radio and listened to the BBC World Service News.

The air smelt of last night's mosquito coil, lying as ash under its small aluminium plinth. Despite the deterrent, one had buzzed by his ear in the middle of the night and fattened itself on his blood. It lingered long enough for him to snap it dead with his hands, its burst carcass staining the netting.

The Ghanaians guarding the barracks kept wood fires going in braziers they'd fashioned from barrels, stood around these at night with their FN rifles slung over their shoulders, chatting with the Lebanese army sentries who showed up on parade most mornings, leaving the soldiering on the streets to the Amal militia.

The Military Police detachment operated from a long building with an eaveless veranda. At ground level the sandbag parapet soaked up rainwater that streamed down the valleys of the corrugated-tin roof. Some of the bags had split, spilling sand, and others were beginning to unstitch. Replacing them would pass the time. Afterwards he'd type up that final traffic accident report and get it off to HQ.

Joe the Fijian was on the Duty Desk this morning, taking weapons in from some French UN soldiers who were visiting the ruins of Tyre. So Harry read last night's journal, checked the ablution area for cleanliness, and the dry toilet for emptiness. He was the on-coming Duty Desk, and if there weren't enough buckets to flush away the waste, the toilet got blocked. Sometimes the off-going Desk didn't bother to replenish the buckets and people just dumped their load and walked away.

Then, if you wanted to crap, you'd to use an Arab toilet and squat over a hole in the tiled basin – it isn't easy to read a newspaper in that position.

Having knocked on the kitchen door he entered. You always knocked beforehand. To let the rats and mice know you were coming in. He checked the cupboard above the sink. If there was a rat or a mouse pinned he'd only have coffee for breakfast. By right he should leave the traps until after breakfast, but that affected his appetite too. He couldn't sit at the oil-cloth-covered table and eat, not with the image of a dead rat next door, black glassy eyes, ringed tail hanging limp, its piss and shit staining the newspaper laid on the shelves. He rapped on the long press and eating a breath swung the double-doors open. Blankety-blank. The trap set, its rasher missing, its blue sewing thread frayed.

Joe said a Ghanaian had eaten the rasher. Probably the rat, too. He didn't like Ghanaians. It was a racist thing with him. He didn't like blacks. He was serious when he said this and he a dusky colour himself. A true Fijian with none of the light colouring that the Indians had brought to the islands. Harry was sure he meant he didn't like Africans but didn't go down the road of asking him. The whole colour issue can raise its ugly head and refuse to lie down. But he derived great craic from the things Joe said to the lads, things no white man who wanted to own wrinkles would ever say: I hate blacks and racists.

That's how the day started. Checking rat traps, eating breakfast, listening to Joe locking the French weapons away. Bitching about the Ghanaians singing jungle songs by the braziers last night, eating the donkey they'd skinned that evening. Going on to say that he'd checked with Ops, and the area of operation was quiet.

Harry sighs, eases the cabinet's drop-leaf down and screws off the brandy top, filling a small glass. Something to hold and swirl, to catch his stare, rather than to drink. The wind moans and dies. Traffic begins to fill the roads, head-beams on.

The radio set crackled with activity. Ops telling the various battalions to go into shelter. Someplace in Nepbatt was hit. He picked up the gist of it as he entered the duty room. Joe was already in flak jacket and helmet, carrying his Sten gun, the Investigation Box sitting at his feet, saying he'd called the others out of their beds to man the desk, and as backup if they need them.

Joe wasn't too sure what had happened, but something had, and Tyre MP had to respond ASAP.

Harry sips hard at his brandy, and tugs on the blind again, revealing the full window picture: beyond the road the Curragh plains flare into a broad expanse of lush green carpet patterned with furze bushes, the last of summer gold on their pine. Grey skies, pylon wires holding chorus lines of birds, racehorses nudged to gallops by jockeys collar-zipped against the cold, a spill of chips, and tree tops of distant woods. He is not in Lebanon, but telling himself that and showing his eyes the proof does not keep the bad dreams away. He bites his lip, fingers sleep crust from his eyes and returns to the armchair.

They drove quickly along the coastal road, passing sand quarries, a half-built hotel – someone's second thought – and twisted railroad tracks that once carried the Orient Express, before wheeling a left turn up Burma Road, hearing gunfire in the distance and the sound of a tank loosening its chamber.

They didn't speak much in the jeep. He drove steadily, not rushing. All he could think about was Ops sending the Battalions into shelter and the MPs out in a soft-top jeep to investigate an incident of which they knew nothing. The unknown mission. It mightn't have been as bad if he'd had time to steel himself. At a checkpoint they were flagged down a narrow, rutted road by Nepalese soldiers. Harry knew the village but its name escaped him. Joe said Kafra. He was right.

He parked in front of the UN post. A Nepalese officer brought them to the scene. A soldier's broken body lay on the ground by a whitewashed wall, his severed right hand beside a railing that guarded an aged olive tree, bullets spilled from his rifle's magazine, its buttstock shattered. And cats darting in and out of the small square, feeding on flesh. An old man carrying a black bag shooing them away, picking up pieces. There was more. Joe touched his ribs to get his attention.

A woman's foot blown off her body sat close to Harry. Upright, blue legging, bone and sinew. Forgotten about in the rush to get her to hospital. The officer had mentioned that, hadn't he? Eighteen years old. She'd a name but it passed by Harry.

The old man's eyes met his. Harry saw a depth of great hurt. The bag opened. Harry Kyle eased to his hunkers, pinched the girl's foot and lowered it into the bag, and watched Joe then go through the same proce-dure with the soldier's hand.

For moments Harry stood there feeling numb in the pit of his belly. Gathering, forcing himself into action, on automatic, he went about his work. Photographed, sketched the murder scene. Names of witnesses for the statements that would be recorded in the coming days. Days of pushing the pen, tapping computer keys, bind-ing the photographs, reading the post-mortem reports – a constant reliving of the nightmare.

On the way back to Tyre they stopped in Nepbatt HQ, and snapped photographs of the deceased. It wasn't his first time to see a dead body. But the others had been of old men and it had seemed sad but natural that they should die.

This was wrong. Bodies torn, the souls wrenched from them. The Nepalese soldier a week left to go home, home to a wife and four-year-old son, who would have only a scant memory of his dad. The young woman …

He'd always known that someday this would happen. That his eyes would be called upon to see such a sight. But he hadn't thought he'd handle it so badly. Didn't think for one moment he'd wake up in a cold sweat, that the sight of bloodied limbs would haunt his nights and his waking hours. Seeing them in the ordinary things he did. Imagining June's foot in a blue legging, seeing the kids missing a hand; horrific thoughts sailing across his mind and sometimes making a return jockey. And cats mewing in his nightmares, craving the taste of human flesh.

The weapons logged in, the blood on his hands and the washing, the constant washing, because his hands can never be clean enough. He tells himself he washes, not because the girl's foot was dirty and covered with the dust of her day, but because he is fearful of being tainted by the evil done to her, but sometimes he acknowledges it is the sight and the feel of her foot he wishes to scrub from his memory.

He hears the door opening, but doesn't look up. Its hinges need oiling. 'Harry?' June says.

His 'Yeah' is low.

'What's wrong?'

He says, 'Nothing.'

'It can't be nothing.'

Tell June?

He and Joe went back to Tyre, rang Ops with their findings and while he typed up a report, Joe sieved kava into a basin and later they drank it, beer too, loads of cheap Lebanese beer. Later getting sick. Harry knowing that his vomiting had nothing to do with his mixing his drinks.

He tells her. Teasing the words out. June waiting for the bits to fall, an eagerness in her blue eyes, as though with his words she could piece him back together, make all the nightmares go away. June's fingers remain on her upper lip. He's finished and he waits for her to say something. Anything. He can tell by her that she doesn't know what to say. Then he catches the smell of that Saturday. It breezes into his nostrils as June says, 'You need to see the doctor, Harry.'

She goes outside to the kids. She meant shrink, he thinks.

The smell grows stronger.

A smell of death, of war, of hell perhaps. And he has a little corner of it, in his mind, all to himself. In the shade – Kafra – his darkest of places.

Something That Happened

Nothing much happens in our town. So when something does occur it seizes the attention of every breathing soul. Like the time Polly Higgins ran away with her biology teacher and Thirsty Tobin was caught dead under the round tower with a half-empty gin bottle growing from his lips. And then the artic that swept too fast round a corner by the wallpaper factory … families stocked up enough cans of beans to last a lifetime.

The ma used to say whenever a wind blew in off the Curragh Plains that it was the Tobins having a farting competition. Right enough, old Thirsty wore a patch on the arse of his trousers. Anyways, don't get me wrong, all these things happened over a span of time, throughout me fourteen years, sort of. Not altogether like what I'm going to tell you. Listen.

Lornie Giles wasn't married. Ma had another word for it. But I thought it sounded cruel. I don't like cruel words. Lornie was a clerk in the general merchants on the town square. Pleasant woman who gave me a Trigger bar when I tolt her her slip was showing. She worked for Thirsty, see. Dang hell, but Thirsty was a hard man. He was big with a thick neck and a crown full of mottled skin. He'd no sense of humour. None. Anyway he was Lornie's boss and the one blamed most for her murder.

I know who kilt her. I tolt Sullivan the guard. He smirked and asked me to feck off. I did, miffed as anything. I never tolt anyone in authority again. Not even at confession to auld Swinney who'd forgiven Thirsty for pissing the candles out in the church. Some say Thirsty paid a whole week's wage to be absolved. No. I'll tell nobody in high places about me secret. What's the point, you know? Lornie's gone and so is the person who done her in.

Lornie was an easy woman to look at. A round face that was smooth with not a lot of make-up on. She smelled like freshly watered roses. A person who smiled. It was a grand summer's evening when Lornie got herself kilt. A lovely red sky was hanging over the chimney pots of the new estate down the lane from our cottage. Not an evening to go getting kilt on.

She was walking her midget hound near a fox cover. A lonely place where the banshees hang around in threes and divils galore hide themselves in the prickly furze. The guards said that Lornie was kilt for her money – two pounds, eleven shillings and a half crown. A lie. Lornie had fourteen pounds and a red ten-bob note. Weren't the guards awful stupid to think that the thief was going to up and disagree with them, eh?

A few people owned up to killing Lornie: Squire Barry who was mad when he wasn't playing Jesus. No Knobs Wilkins who claimed the reward, and Mrs Coady who admitted that she wanted to kill Lornie for a long time and had been sleepwalking the evening of the murder.

Of course, none of them done it. Around that time Polly Higgins came home without her teacher but with a bump on her tummy.

'Left me in Dublin on me tod,' she whinged, 'only I've news for him next time I see him.' Her eyes danced. 'This isn't his baby. No.'

The place hushed up, you know. Folk reckoned that Mr Teacher got suspicious about Thirsty (an old flame of Polly's). Anyway, people held on to the girl's words like they were pearls falling from her mouth. Polly emphasised proudly, 'The babby isn't that creep's.'

'Whose then?' asked the old woman Coady, a finger at her nose.

Polly shot her a dose of venom. 'Ah, how would I know. All those beans you ate … Did you ever know which one of them made you fart?'

Boy, some reply, huh? Anyway the baby was Thirsty's and he weren't too happy when Mrs Thirsty got wind of it.

Mass, the Sunday after Lornie was found, was a solemn affair. The Blackmailer, Fr Swinney, was an auld grouch. He gave a leathering sermon, saying that the murderer could even be among us at this very moment in the house of God, eyeing up his next victim. Waiting to pounce and throttle the life out of some poor eejit. Not alone was Lornie a murder victim, now she was just a poor eejit to boot. Garda Sullivan squiggled his big arse on the pew, the fat rolling over his trouser belt. He'd twigged something and slapped the handcuffs on Swinney when Mass finished.

Sullivan's face was flushed with triumph. He came out of the sacristy pushing Swinney in front of him. The priest still wearing his vestments. It later emerged that the guards had not released details of how Lornie got kilt. Sullivan hadn't banked on Swinney making a genuine assumption. Later, the guard had his choice of barracks in the remotest parts of Ireland.

After dinner I met the killer walking his dog through the park. We knew each other. And I stopped to talk with him. He lived on the other side of town with a tramp called Delia. I asked him out straight, why did he kill Lornie? He just gave me a baleful look, you know like, and said it was an accident. All the while looking around like he was figuring on doing me in. So I legged it, vowing never to talk to him on my own again. He was rat slim with a high brainy forehead and oily black hair. His fingers were long and slender. Dangerous, with a mind of their own. How could he kill her, eh? An accident? No way. Didn't I see him? But like I said, nobody believed me.

Me da was up to his tricks again. Not paying the maintenance, like. The bastard had a good job, too. A judge. Aye, a hard one at that. Miserable he was, in nature and appearance. Anyway, I got to thinking about the reward of one hundred pounds. The right figure to cheer the ma up. Yeah, Ma wouldn't speak to me. A cloud of depression had settled on her and not a word would she utter. So I got myself to barracks … again. For the ultimate time.

Yer man behind the counter with the mugs of tea on it wasn't really a guard. He was denser looking than Sullivan. I took him to be a detective, like. You would. He listened to me as if I had a screw loose and then said, 'Go home, ya little gobshite.'

Huffed, I started to walk way. My ears picked up another voice.

'Hey Bill, come on, clean this mess up before the inspector arrives.'

A guard. A real one. I turned, but the two of them were giggling at me. Shag them, I thought. I'll tell no one anymore. I was so maddened I went to see Da's hussy when he was at court.

She was a grand woman, all right. She's long eyelashes that Ma said were false and a huge chest that Ma hoped was false. She wore clothes that stuck to her like jam to bread. She had a beauty spot on the angle of her jaw. You could have skied on the makeup. She gave me a fiver once. Yeah, I found her and Da on the leather sofa in the front room. She was kissing him on the lips and he wasn't doing a whole lot to stop her. I asked for a tenner. Well, you've got to know what a secret's worth, haven't you? In the long run I settled for the fiver, figuring that the secret was going to blow sooner rather than later. It did. Seems the ma discovered a pair of French knickers around the ears of our Saint Martin statue. Furious she was. I felt for her. It's not right seeing your ma crying.

I imagined a glimmer of red on the statue's cheeks. But with his face as dark as the entrance to a train tunnel I couldn't swear to it. But the statue did move, certainly – right over Da's head. Something about the knickers caught me eye. But the ma rushed me into burning them, and I couldn't fully check them out. It all clicked with me later though.

The next morning Thirsty was discovered dead. He'd gone on a super binge when his missus was tolt by Lornie about Polly's baby. Mrs Thirsty went apeshit and threw him out. The guards appeared to lose interest in finding Lornie's killer after that. So they never got their man. Soon people forgot about Lornie, the way they do when a person is dead a while. Ma got over the French knickers episode.

'So what if she's into them,' she said, putting a brave face on. It hurt more to think that Da was also.

Anyway, going on. The da's hussy was mortified when I went to see her. She was disgusted over him not paying us any money. The other news took longer to sink in. You see, me da used to do a line with Lornie. I knew because I had my suspicions riled up and followed him about. I was talking with Lornie the evening she got kilt. About how, you know, me ma would die if she knew the da had another woman on top of the extra one he already had.

Well. Lornie and Da had a right row. Both their dogs ran away. I couldn't pull his hand off her throat. His mind seemed to be elsewhere, like, he could have been shaking his tail after a pee. Choking someone nary fizzled him a bit. He kilt Lornie dead. In a way I was as bad: I took her money, but only because I was looking for something smelly in her handbag to revive her. Not even a whiff of a camel's fart would have brought Lornie around. The da skited off, brushing his hands casually in his slacks and then patting his hound.

'She'll be OK,' he said, short of cheerfully.

Talk about famous last words.

So, I kept my mouth clamped. The da coughed up his money and more besides. Sometimes the knowledge burdened me, especially when I needed the money to go somewhere special. Delia took her tramping else-where. Never did see her again. I placed flowers on Lornie's grave. Got lovely roses from her next-door neighbour in the cemetery. I mean, Lornie deserved them more than anyone. Not a lot of murdered dead people in that place. Feel bad about taking her money. But those were hungry times for the ma and me and I'm sure Lornie understands.

I should, like, have tolt Lornie to keep away from Da. I saw da go vacant in the face before when he tried to strangle Ma. And he would have done, only I stuck a breadknife in his arse. Pity I couldn't find something similar for Lornie.

Yeah, I finally made up my mind to turn Da in when he sentenced Thirsty as the killer in a fancy restaurant one night. It wasn't a courtroom, OK, but it might as well have been, with all the top judges and the like there. I was listening, you see, me brand new first job. His eyes did a jig when he saw me and realised I'd heard. He died a day later. Took one of those apoplectic fits when I whispered into his ear, 'Da, that was Lornie's French knickers Ma found in the sitting room, you know. She's still trying to match the initials on them, putting two and two together, like.'

His eyes were fiery. Then he composed himself and said laughingly, 'Drinks for my companions – that's what I said, boy …'

'For a devil's toast,' I shouted, and left to look for a new job – the da taking his leave of this life. I hope Lornie gives him hell.

The Head of God

Suntan Reilly lives in Flat 4 in a nameless lane. A squalid habitat where at night in his bed he hears mice at play in the attic. He is about sixty, has salt and pepper hair, a pot belly. He doesn't care for where he is or the struggle ahead.

In his flat there are a TV, radio, kettle, a coffee pot with chipped spout, a sandwich toaster, a deep fat fryer, a bowl of oranges, some mouldy, and a stack of old newspapers he uses to soak up the wet that seeps under the front door during bouts of heavy rainfall.

Most mornings he wakens early, listens to the radio and makes himself a mug of strong tea. He sits at a small oil-clothed table by the window in order to catch the paltry light.

His front door is parallel to the cathedral's high curtain wall and out back there is a tiny jungle, wild before he assumed tenancy.

If it's a dry morning he will walk the lanes to the park, carrying a beige shopping bag. Most mornings the park is empty. Occasionally there is a man who walks an Alsatian, but he keeps to the end close to the railway tracks.

This morning is dry, so Suntan takes the smallish blue football from the bag and drops it at his feet and sets to kicking it ahead of him. There is no set pattern to his efforts; he follows the ball, his hands behind his back, torso bent slightly forward as though he were facing into a stiff breeze.

There is a face drawn on the ball in thick black indelible marker: eyes, eyebrows, nose, teeth and ears. The ears are tiny dots – he believes this signifies the football's deafness. A thin line passes for lips caught in a broad smile.

He has lived in the town for about a year. He knew no one when he came and he knows no one now. If someone asks his name he says it is Suntan. Saying this appears to confirm something in the other's eyes, and there is a hurried retreat back to wherever.

His real name is Charles Reilly. He is of the Reillys who used to live in a village just inside the Dublin border. That is Reilly – without a preceding O or apostrophe.

Every Thursday brings a visitor. He does not permit her to visit him in his flat. She is a woman who steps from a bus at the Market Square and crosses the busy road at a set of traffic lights, where the green figure is slow to appear and quick to disappear. Her name is Nancy. She is roughly the same age as Suntan, has bad rosacea, is of stout build and strong disposition.

Meanwhile Suntan has left the park and is already seated in the café where he is to meet Nancy. He is never late for their appointment.

He orders white coffee and a hot fruit scone from a young woman with a receding chin and an impolite cast to her features. He has noticed the look is only visible whenever she serves him, those like him and coloured people.

'Regular or medium?' she says.

He always orders regular. She knows this.

He says, 'Regular.'

He glances now and then at the café's red door. The door has tall glass panels and he can see some of the street through them. Just inside the entrance there is a coatstand and a large terracotta urn that brims with copper-tinted shrubs.

When the girl returns he notices a little spillage on the saucer and the absence of a complimentary biscuit. Irrespective of whether he orders a scone or a Danish pastry he always gets a biscuit, a ginger snap wrapped in cellophane. Perhaps the café is out of them, or this is her way of saying that she does not like him. She might want him to ask for it. Though it's more probable that she thinks what he has to say doesn't matter, counts for very little. Also, she knows that he is not the sort to protest. He espies Nancy through the glass in the door. Once inside, she will glance at the silver watch he knows she has looked at five minutes before, as the bus lurched to a stop with a squeal of brakes and a slight shudder.

Nancy ventures a contrived smile when she sees him. She joins him at his alcove table, slips off her scarf with a magician's flourish and then removes her coat, draping both over the back of her chair. She says it looks like rain.

He says the forecast is for squalls.

She asks how he is.

'I'm fine.'

He catches the scent of her perfume, her facial cream. Remembers the odour of her perspiration, of a kitchen that stank of boiling cabbage, of darkness pressing its weight against the windows of their parents' old country home. The girl arrives at Nancy's side and asks if she'd like to order. There is no cast to her features. Nancy orders her usual, please. She says, 'Usual,' and the girl writes without having to query. It is not lost on Suntan that he frequents the premises far more often than his twin.

He is glad that Nancy has given up trying to convince him that he is better. She used to say that he was looking well in himself. In spite of his not having washed and shaven for a week.

He sips at his coffee and cuts his scone and butters the halves. Nancy asks if he wants jam. He shakes his head. He wants to eat the scone before it cools. It doesn't make sense to order something hot and then wait to eat it cold.

Nancy mentions her husband, Aaron. How well he's coming on after his operation. How good her grandson is. Every time they pass a church he reminds her to bless herself. He serves Mass, you know. The longer she talks the more of a strain it becomes for her. It is as though her heart is running out of hope for him, is sputtering to a halt like a car with a needle deep in the red. She tries though.

'His old terrier is poorly,' Nancy says, pushing the car now.

He imagines Sophie with her bent ears, letting the wind freshen her face.

'Charles,' she says, when the girl delivering her tea and toasted cheese sandwich has departed.

'I hope you're not going to start, Nance.'

'I just want you to be happy. It's killing me to see you like this.'

'I'm on the mend.'

'The dirt is falling off you.'

'I was always a dirty colour.'

'Shave, buy yourself new clothes, come and live with me.'

'No.'

'We could build a granny flat for you – our garden's big enough. You could help Aaron to build it. The exercise would be good for him and you.'

'No.'

She sighs, puts her hand to her lips, touches the flange of her ear, a habit she brought with her from childhood.

'We were always so close,' she says.

'We still are, Nance.'

'I could kill that woman.'

She means Babs. She means what she says.

Nancy fails to understand that his depression is his depression. Caused by no one except himself, his awry genetics, chromosomes, whatever. He wants to tell her this but refrains. If she wants to blame Babs for his mental health, then that is her business.

'You gave her everything. You forgave her every time. You were too good for her.'

'Nance, please.'

'I'm sorry. I just get so mad when I think about her.'

Does she really believe that he has fallen to these depths because of Babs: the lovers she took, her drunkenness, her vile tongue, her hard-heartedness? Sure he felt rage, pain, a heartache that even now and then comes to him like blurts of a cutting wind. But, no. Babs merely took him down a flight or two, not all the way to the basement floor. The lift is broken, so he's taking the stairs. From where he's standing it's a long way up.

'What are you doing with yourself?' Nancy asks.

He has an every-week answer to this every-week question.

'Not much. I walk a lot, read plenty, make sure I take the right pills at the correct time.'

'How long more, Charles, is this going to go on for?'

He shrugs. Well, he doesn't know. There has to be a turning point somewhere. He is some way up the stairwell – there's no easy climb.

When he says this, she nods, apparently content that he is at least going to sink no deeper into the quagmire.

'I don't like being this far down,' he says.

'I know that. Everyone knows that,' Nancy says, freshening her cup.

'People treat you differently when you're in this part of the woods,' he says.

'How? In what way?'

'In a blaming way – tinged with contempt and a little hatred.'

'Ah, Charles, people are very good. It's not like the old days – the stigma isn't …'

'Is it? Gone? You think? I see it in some people, in how they look at me. It's like I'm less human than they are.'

'Come home with me.'

'Nance – no. But thanks.'

'At least let me help with money?'

'Nance …'

'You were mad to leave *her* in that lovely house. She has everything and you have nothing.'

'I have something, Nance. I have me. Me.'

There's something cryptic in her eyes, her tiny smile. She reaches out a hand and covers his.

'Right now that isn't enough – that's why God gave you a twin.'

'God,' he spits.

He walks the park. It drizzles. He kicks the ball ahead of him. It is a tired ball, softening.

This ball is not the Lamb of God: it is the Head of God.

He kicks it as a release from the strife in his life, for the suffering he and others like him endure, for the victims of war and famine, for the murder victims, for the poor. He drives the ball farthest when he thinks of the slick people in their slick motors who drive by children who sleep in church porches. He kicks against the unfairness of it all.

This morning is different however. The man and his Alsatian are in the park, forced out of their routine by the builders who have moved onto the site of the tennis club.

The dog chases the ball, takes it in his mouth, squeezes and lets it fall. He scampers through the gates of the park; his bespectacled owner, giving chase, glances behind and pants an apology.

Suntan walks to his ball. It is squashed, riven with holes and washed in dog saliva.

'Even the dogs are pissed off with Ya,' he says.

He admires the bite of the dog.

The next morning Suntan Reilly orders a white coffee. Regular, he says. The young woman runs her eyes over his suitcase. The new football with the fresh indelible-inked features sits in the palm of his hand.

'Do you like him?' he says.

'It's a ball, just a ball,' she says.

He tells her it's more than that. It's something to blame.

'Therapeutic?' she says.

And of course this is true.

He has turned on, if not towards, his God. And isn't that, in its own paradoxical way, a display of belief? She forgets his biscuit and there's a spillage in his saucer. He stares hard for a long time at what's in front of him.

Calls her back.

A Change of Energy

All that June week I'd been bothered about whether or not to do the right thing. Deep down I wanted the bad thing so much. So we got round to doing it and later I wished I had the choice back, but there was no hope of that, so I had to face into what was next.

When you get to my age you begin to think that whatever you thought you were missing in life had passed you by and you may just as well settle down and see the days out to meet whatever it is that will rip you from this world.

I've been married to Kate for about twenty-seven years and mostly we get along fine. Our sons live in the States and we go over there about every two years to visit. We don't have grandchildren, yet. The boys married career-minded women who don't have time for the grinning and bearing to do with parenting. I can't say that I blame a woman for putting off the pains. If I were a woman, I doubt very much if I'd go too willingly down that road.

We married young, if you consider twenty-two to be

young. And we've had our ups and downs like most couples, like the time Kate was almost wrote off in a car accident and her shoulder was wrecked. It took her a long time to get over that and I'm not too sure if she ever fully recovered. We broke up for a couple of weeks a few years ago, about as long as we could bear to be apart from each other, and I can't even remember now what that argument was about, but I'm fairly sure that it had to do with money or her mother. Both, maybe. Too little of one and too much of the other. At the time I suppose each of us felt we'd put down a marker to the other about something. What exactly that marker was, neither of us was too sure – there are some feelings and more thoughts that you simply can't excavate with words.

Until a week or so ago I used to work at the race-horses in a small yard that hadn't turned out a winner in four years. My boss, Mister Joseph Cornell, inherited big money from his father who supplied X-ray machines to hospitals throughout the world. He keeps about eight jumpers and four flat horses, and about a month ago he brought in a two-year-old in the hope that a new arrival might bring in a change of energy and luck. This horse is a handsome chestnut with four white socks and a white blaze and they called him Sammy's Darling.

As it was, the horses that were of some use weren't sound; the best of them was never going to leave his lameness behind. And the sound ones were too slow to enter in a race. When a stable isn't turning out winners you get to live on a flat week's wage. That's the curse of it. Down the years I could have gone to a couple of other stables for a little more money and probably three or four horses to care for, which, if they won, would have brought in a bonus. But when you've been a head lad, even of a small stable, you don't really ever fancy taking orders from another head lad because it'd be like the blood pumping backwards in you. I've been in the same yard under three different owners – I haven't worked anywhere else in all my thirty-two-year working life. I guess there is such a thing as being married to the job.

I became a jump jockey after the first five years; in about eight seasons I rode thirty-seven winners – not a great tally, but I know guys with much worse who've gone on to do far better than me. I had to quit riding because of my weight; had gotten fed up sweating off the ounces and taking those pills that help pregnant women to piss. I'm sure there's a payday for me somewhere down the line for the broken bones, the constant dieting, haemorrhaging of sweat and the pills.

A young lad called Skinny McHugh was the only other full-timer there. He had a past that limited his options regarding work, but I found him all right. Not much of a talker and he had this way of looking at you sidelong when he was reproached. I didn't ever have much reason to do that, mind, and when I did, I kept civility in my tone so that he knew that I respected him and appreciated having him about because of the good work that he did. Also, I didn't especially want to find out what was at the other end of that sidelong look.

The two of us rode our charges to the gallops in the mornings, two lots, and an old guy called Harry Salford helped out part-time. He worked in a garage in the afternoons. He was talking about cutting down on his workload, without saying which end he was going to surrender. But I know he loves horses better than he does cars and people and the fact that he said he was a morning person made me hope he'd be with us a while yet.

Harry talks too much, that's his fault, and he tells you the same things over and over, which doesn't make him a bar buddy of anybody. But he balanced out Skinny's long silences and too-short sentences when he did decide to exercise his tongue.

My trouble started about ten days ago, and the thing with trouble is that you often don't recognise it at first sight. Mister Cornell said he'd bought this lovely chestnut colt, that I've already mentioned, for a patron of the yard, a Mrs Andrea Doolin who wanted to work there for a couple of months to give her something to do. It seemed she had come out of a very long illness and wanted to relive her youth when she worked for a time in a Newmarket yard. Her husband, Ivor Doolin, is a big buddy of Mister Cornell's.

She's about my age, no height to her. Fair-haired and pale and sharp-faced, with a harsh voice that has a trace of impatience in it, like a wind sneaking in through a gap. She's the sort of woman who doesn't like to hang about or be left hanging about when she makes up her mind that she wants something. She married well, but divorced and then married Ivor.

These things she told me in the tack room by the saddle stalls. We were sipping at mugs of beef-and-onion soup as Harry and Skinny sat close to the gas heater that only breathed on one bar. It was milling rain and a wind was rising and the three of us had come in wet-faced from the gallops. Andrea had ridden one of the slowcoaches, and I'd been on an even slower animal. Skinny had taken the chestnut, and while he liked the horse, I could tell he didn't care much for Andrea – there was an added ingredient in his sidelong look at her.

Resentment, I made out, but Andrea didn't appear to notice. Anyhow, we got along well and when the guys were gone home we'd be in the tack room and within a week, I suppose, we kissed and this led to the placing of horse blankets on the floor between the saddle stalls. And I don't know, but it seemed so right to be sliding inside her and wherever my conscience was, it must have relocated, for I suffered no pangs – and that's what I had been doing behind my wife's back, stirring up trouble with my prick.

Maybe mine is a slow-working conscience, and don't get me wrong, there's no fear of me spilling my guts and owning up to Kate. That'd be a cruel thing to do to her, and even though some would probably admire the honesty, I think it's cowardly. I found myself looking at Kate and thinking how she'd stuck with me over the years, and that if she knew I'd poked a woman ten years younger than her and a whole lot prettier she would be cut to the heart. And whenever I saw her smile and the ordinary pleasantness of her face I cringed inside, thinking how she was a mere few spoken words from being unhappy. So, I made up my mind to tell Andrea I had to quit, and she understood, but we went one last time at it, and that was Skinny's undoing, and mine as far as my job was concerned.

You think that you can put this into place to change that, or return to the way you were before, but sometimes fate and people make that impossible. Skinny had been looking at us the time before, using a video recorder. We didn't hear him come in or leave, till we were done and tidy in our clothes and the only giveaway clue was our red cheeks. He came in without knocking, gave us a sidelong look each and said he had something to show us. He flipped out the side-viewer and pressed Play, turning the camera about to let us watch ourselves on the tiny screen.

He had a copy made, he said, 'So don't go trying any funny stuff. It's with a mate.'

Funny stuff is what he actually said. He'd bluffed. Some people just can't do bluff. Andrea asked him what he wanted and he smiled and said not much, and mentioned a figure that she scoffed at, and said that she didn't care what he did with the video or who saw it or didn't.

'Away you go,' she said, walking past him, opening the door and walking through it. Well, Skinny spent a few seconds reeling in the slack to his chin. He owned fool's gold. Then he cheered in himself because he still had me, only I shook my head and said I was like Andrea, didn't give two blind fucks what he did with it. But that he could take himself out of the yard right now. This was easier said than done because Skinny lived in a mobile home on Mister Cornell's land.

'Your missus?' he said.

'You grab your things and get out. You can do what you like with the video, but I'll do you for attempted blackmail.'

I could see by him that he wanted to roll the dice back to square one, but there was no doing that for him either. Then he sort of gave in on himself and tears came to him and he said he owed for drug money and they were putting pressure on him to pay up. I didn't know till then that he had a drug habit. The things the eyes miss.

At that moment Harry walked in saying there was a breeze out there that would cut the hole off you as he went over to the Burco that was a minute off coming to the boil.

'Sorry, did I walk in on something?' he said.

'No,' I said.

Then he saw the camcorder and said they were a great yoke altogether, that he'd videoed his grand-daughter's First Communion, brilliant invention.

'Have you anything on yours worth seeing?' Harry said.

Skinny said, 'No,' and popped the release catch and handed me the cassette. 'There's no copy.'

I sighed and said, 'Fine.'

Skinny looked at me like he was asking me for something.

'You apologise to Andrea and we'll talk later.'

When I was gone I moved my eyes from the door to Harry and said, 'They had words.'

'About the chestnut?'

'Yeah, she said he was too rough with him.'

'He was a little. He's got things on his mind.'

Harry wore a green quilted jacket with leather elbow-patches and a corduroy collar that he kept raised as though the edges of his ears were always cold. He came over close to me, hands buried deep in his pockets. A pocket of blackheads nested close to the bridge of his nose had me wondering why they were there – had no one ever said anything of them to him, or why hadn't he noticed for himself in the mirror? He was always a bit dirty in himself but I didn't fully realise it till that moment – I guess my senses had been heightened by the business with Skinny. Harry smelled of piss and I remembered him telling me that his tap was leaking. I'd wanted to ask if he'd been to the doctor with that yet but hadn't because I was selfish, see, I didn't want him going sick and putting an extra workload on us. I was surprised to find myself thinking like that – lately I've been giving myself loads of surprises.

He pinched his nose then and said in a low voice, 'He's in big trouble with the drug lads.'

'I gathered as much.'

'Jesus, yeah, he owes them boys a fucking fortune.'

'How much?'

'He told me €7,000.'

'Fuck.'

'An expensive habit – if he's not snorting, he's smoking and popping pills to beat the band.'

'Why didn't you tell me this before now?'

He backed away a couple of steps, a 'there's-gratitude-for-you' look in his eyes, and said, 'Amn't I after telling you?'

'Sooner?' I said.

'Sooner? I told you as soon as I could – twice I came in here this last week and the noise of the humping was unreal – would yous not think to lock the door?'

My mind went blank.

'Alright getting your hole, but ye're married and don't need to be caught at it.'

'Harry.'

'Don't mind me – I don't give a flying fuck what grown-ups do indoors to each other.'

Then he said he knew lots of people in town who went around as though they had two full wings stuck to their backs, and truth be known about them, they hadn't a fucking feather to tickle themselves with.

'So, you remember that – you're flying on one wing.'

I didn't see Andrea for a couple of days after that. When she arrived in, she wasn't dressed for work but for business, and she talked to me like what we had done was a million miles and a thousand years distant. She wanted to know how her horse was doing, said that she would be running the place for a week as Mister and Mrs Cornell were going to Florida. I'd already been told that but not about Andrea living in their house in their absence.

'You don't have a problem with that?' she said. We were alone in the tack room.

'No.'

'Good.'

'Only …'

'Yes?'

'I burned the cassette.'

'Cassette …'

Her face was blank for a second, then puzzled.

'Skinny,' I said.

'Oh, that?'

She smiled. And like Skinny's sidelong smile I didn't care much for what lay the far side of it.

Two nights later I took a call from Andrea. She said there was a fire in the yard and the fire brigade was on its way and that I should come out. There were horses needed settling and I thought of the smoke and fear they were enduring and I remembered the scene of a stable fire that I'd once visited and it was the most God-awful fucking thing I'd ever witnessed – dead horses, the smell of roasted horse flesh and singed hair stuck to my nostrils for weeks. When I got to the yard the horses were OK. Harry had responded quickest, riding in on what he calls his super scooter – he lives a half-mile away – and moved them into the paddock before the fire took hold in the stables.

I saw the mobile home, what was left of it, a mound of smouldering ash, the fire crew's yellow hoses like snakes spewing out thick jets of water; heard the irritating drone of the pumps and smelt the rubbery and oily smells.

Andrea and her husband stood talking to a guard. She spotted me and beckoned me over and I gave the policeman all I knew about Skinny.

They never found any sign of human remains. Yet what little money Skinny had in his bank account hasn't been touched. His relatives haven't accepted that he possibly died in the blaze – the forensic people said there was an accelerant used but I pointed out that the mobile had had a kerosene heater. Still.

Anyway, I believe Skinny's dead. Though I don't think he died in the fire. No. I think he was maybe dead before smoke and flame got near him.

I left the job shortly afterwards, just couldn't bear to hang around the place. Andrea and her smile, you know. Harry quit too. And I hear the new foreman is tall and young and handsome.

Mister Cornell said he understood why I was leaving and didn't try to talk me out of it. He gave me a good reference and a bit of a bonus. He could have afforded to do that to begin with, but these days he has extra dough since the chestnut had gone on to win three races on the trot. The things that a change of energy can bring about.